Spellbound Sugar

Ashley MacKinnon

ISBN: 978-1-970296-00-6

Dedication

I've never appreciated more the small enchantments that turn the everyday into something extraordinary. From the scent of fresh bread, the glow of candlelight, to the hush of stories shared at dusk everything carries more weight now. May this book be a companion for quiet hours and a reminder that even the simplest moments can carry a touch of magic.

Chapter 1 – Flour and Magic

The scent of browned butter and sugar clung to the rafters of *The Golden Spoon,* wrapping the little bakery in a warmth that no lamp or hearth could quite rival. Evening was the quietest time here when the bustle of customers faded into a hum of memory and Morgana Valehart was left alone with her ingredients, thoughts, and secrets.

She wiped her flour-dusted palms against her apron then reached for the sack of sugar at the end of the counter. The wooden countertop was worn smooth with years of kneading, chopping, and whisking with generations of baking etched into every groove. Morgana inhaled, savoring the faint sweetness of vanilla still lingering in the air from the morning's pastries.

Perfect time for a little experimenting.

The Golden Spoon wasn't hers technically. Agnes and Tomas Fairbairn, the bakery's owners, were the ones who held the deed and signed the orders for flour and eggs. They were kind people, gray-haired and gentle. They were the sort who loved telling stories as much as feeding their customers. They'd taken Morgana on not only for her skill, but for her relentless curiosity and her way of making familiar recipes feel new. They knew she was *different*. They even knew she practiced a little magic here and there. What mattered most to them was that she never let it creep into the food they sold at the front counter.

That was the rule. No spells in the bread, no enchantments in the pies, no charms tucked inside flaky croissants.

The Fairbairns said the rule had stood for half a century ever since a witch across town enchanted her loaves to keep customers coming back. At first no one realized. But soon people noticed they had no appetite for any bread but hers and anger grew when choice was stolen from them. The bakery closed in disgrace and the lesson hardened into law: food must never carry magic.

But tonight was just for her.

She opened a jar of cinnamon and let the warm spice tickle her nose then slid it back onto the shelf. Too strong for what she wanted. Her gaze lingered on a row of small vials tucked at the far end of the spice rack with their contents glinting faintly in the low lamplight. The average eye would have seen nothing but an assortment of dusty bottles. But to Morgana they shimmered faintly. They had an aura of potential humming in the air around them.

She brushed her fingertips across the glass feeling the pulse of each one. Passionflower. Rosehip. A pinch of dried clover. She smiled to herself. The ingredients weren't dangerous on their own. Not unless combined with care, intention, and focus. Which of course she had in spades.

"Chocolate chip cookies," she murmured to herself while setting out a bowl. "Nothing suspicious about that."

The words made her grin. Everyone loved chocolate chip cookies. They were comforting, reliable, and sweet. The perfect canvas for a tiny test.

She cracked two eggs into the bowl with their yolks glowing golden in the faint lamplight. The butter was already softened and the sugar measured. With smooth practiced movements she began to cream the mixture together while humming softly under her breath. Her magic stirred with her rhythm as natural to her as the beat of her heart.

Just a trace, she thought letting her focus slip to the little vial of rosehip. *Nothing anyone would notice. Nothing harmful.*

Magic in its rawest form was hungry. It wanted to root itself in whatever vessel it could find and to twine around emotions and memories like ivy curling up a stone wall. Morgana had spent years learning to coax it, to keep it obedient, and to fold it into her craft instead of letting it swallow her whole.

Tonight she asked it for warmth. For affection. It was a harmless charm that was meant to encourage kindness and fondness among those who tasted it.

She tipped a pinch of the rosehip powder into the dough while whispering the words under her breath. The syllables glowed in her mind's eye like faint sparks and weaving threads of power into the butter and sugar. She added the flour, the chocolate chips, and then the baking soda. Stirred clockwise then counterclockwise. Pressed her palm flat over the bowl as if blessing it.

And the dough *shivered.* Not the gentle settling she'd intended. It *pulsed* like a heartbeat finding its rhythm. The air around the bowl grew warm then hot. It carried a scent that wasn't quite cinnamon. It was like something sharper. Headier. The kind of sweetness that made you dizzy if you breathed it too long.

Morgana stepped back. Love magic was notoriously unstable. Every practitioner knew that. It fed on the emotions already present and then amplified them beyond the caster's control. Her mother had warned her once. "Loneliness and longing are dangerous fuels. They burn hotter than you expect."

Morgana frowned. The hum of magic in the air had changed. It seemed richer and thicker now. Not dangerous exactly, but more than she'd intended.

Hmm. Maybe the rosehip was fresher than I thought.

She hesitated for half a breath then shrugged. A test was a test. She rolled the dough into neat balls and arranged them on a parchment-lined tray. The oven was already hot and filling the room with a steady glow. She slid the tray inside and closed the door.

The timer clicked into place and Morgana leaned against the counter. She brushed stray flour from her hair.

That was when the front bell chimed.

She jumped up and then nearly knocked over a jar of sugar. *Who in the world—?* The bakery was closed and the front doors locked an hour ago.

She wiped her hands quickly on her apron and stepped into the front room.

A tall figure stood silhouetted in the doorway framed by the twilight spilling in through the glass. His coat was dusted with road grime and his boots were worn from travel. And though his dark hair had grown longer since she'd last seen him and his jaw was shadowed with stubble Morgana recognized him instantly.

Evander Grimshaw.

Her breath caught. She pressed a hand to her sternum and felt her pulse hammer against her palm.

He looked older. Sharper. But those storm-gray eyes were the same. They were eyes that missed nothing and had once unsettled her even as they drew her closer.

"Morgana," he said with his voice low and smooth as velvet stretched over steel. "Didn't think I'd find you here."

For a moment she forgot how to breathe.

Evander Grimshaw of all people. Here. Now.

"What are you doing in Eraldor?" she asked with her voice steadier than she felt.

He stepped further inside with the bell jingling again as the door shut behind him. "Work. Business. Passing through. And I heard there was a little bakery on the corner that made the best bread in the city."

Her lips twitched despite herself. "We're closed."

He tilted his head. His smile was faint but unmistakable. "So I'll settle for conversation."

Morgana awkwardly laughed as she tried to hide the sudden heat in her cheeks. "It's late Evander."

"Never too late for old acquaintances." His gaze flicked briefly toward the kitchen. "You're baking something."

The scent of cookies wafted through the air betraying her.

"It's nothing," she said quickly. "Just... leftovers."

He rested one shoulder against the wall. It looked casual, but there was always a quiet intensity to him. It was the kind of thing that made it feel like he was seeing straight through her. "I'll take your word for it. Unless of course you're offering."

The oven timer dinged.

Morgana froze.

Evander raised a single eyebrow. "Perfect timing."

She cursed silently while hurrying back into the kitchen. The cookies were golden brown and their chocolate chips were melted to glossy pools. They smelled heavenly and the magic humming in them was stronger now and totally unmistakable. She swallowed.

This is fine. They're just cookies. A tiny spell nothing more. He won't even notice.

But her pulse quickened as she lifted the tray. She set it on the counter to cool with the sweet scent filling every corner of the room. Evander followed her lingering in the doorway like a shadow she couldn't shake.

"They smell… incredible," he said.

She busied herself with a spatula, sliding the cookies onto a rack. "Don't get any ideas. These aren't for sale."

He reached out faster than she could stop him and plucked one from the tray.

"Evander—"

Too late. He bit into it.

The world seemed to still.

Magic rippled like a shiver through the air tugging at the edges of her consciousness. Morgana's heart dropped into her stomach. The threads she had woven into the dough were unraveling now and wrapping themselves around Evander like a cloak.

He closed his eyes for a moment savoring the bite then opened them again. And when his gaze landed on her something had changed.

Warmer. Brighter. Dangerous.

Her breath caught.

No, no, no. This isn't right. That was supposed to be subtle. Just a nudge. Not this.

Evander smiled faintly. It was slow and deliberate. "You've outdone yourself Morgana."

She forced a laugh. "It's just a cookie."

But his eyes lingered on her like she was the only thing in the room worth noticing.

Morgana turned back to the counter with her mind racing now.

The spell had worked too well. And now unless she could undo it Evander Grimshaw was walking proof that she'd broken the bakery's one unshakable rule.

No magic in the food. No exceptions.

And yet here he was.

And here she was.

And the night was only beginning.

Chapter 2 – The Handsome Customer

The morning rush at *The Golden Spoon* was a kind of symphony. From the clink of porcelain cups, the scrape of chairs across wooden floors, the low buzz of conversation, and the warm hiss of steam as Tomas pulled shots of espresso behind the counter. Sunlight filtered through lace curtains turning the air golden and dust-speckled. The smell of fresh bread wafted in steady waves mingling with cinnamon rolls and fruit tarts lined neatly in their glass cases. A warm haze of yeast and sugar curled through the air and welcomed customers.

There was always a big variety of patrons who came into the bakery. Two dockworkers were in before their shift. They were hunched over mugs of coffee talking softly together despite their large size. Their boots were leaving small wet marks on the floor. It was impossible to avoid the puddles from the earlier rainstorm. Near them was a very frazzled looking mother trying desperately to bribe her young son with a sticky bun. The boy looked barely four years old and was throwing a massive tantrum, drawing looks from other patrons. Every now and then the mother would cast nervous glances at the patrons and immediately focused back on her yelling son.

Morgana Valehart moved swiftly between counter and oven. Her hands were dusted with flour and her apron smudged with chocolate. Her long braid swung behind her as she carried out trays of muffins to refill the shelves. On the surface she looked every bit the busy baker's assistant. But beneath her calm smile she was knotted with nerves.

Unbidden a warning from one of her previous magical mentors came to the front of her mind. He always told her to "never let magic touch the tongue. Desire is the hardest spell to undo." She was definitely feeling that warning more deeply now.

She remembered the clumsy spells of her late teens. Potions were brewed with too much longing and charms were whispered without her full focus. A love charm once had the whole village baker chasing after a farmer's wife for a week before she managed to undo it. After that incident Morgana was red-faced and shaken. Another time a simple warming spell had flared out of control nearly setting her clothes alight. Each mistake had etched a quiet fear into her bones. Magic born from hunger or haste always carried a cost.

The memory of last night lingered like a too strong perfume. Every glance and every word between them replayed in sharp fragments leaving her feeling restless.

I should have thrown them out. Should've kept him from taking even a single bite.

But Evander Grimshaw had eaten one of her enchanted cookies. Then another. And when he looked at her something in his eyes had burned too brightly and too intently like embers catching flame.

She'd barely slept replaying every glance and every word. Magic was tricky enough when contained. Unchecked it had a way of spiraling beyond her control.

She forced herself to focus on arranging blueberry muffins and pressing them into neat rows. *It's fine. He'll be gone by now. Just passing through the city, he said. Maybe I'll never even see him again.*

The front bell jingled.

Her heart dropped straight into her stomach.

There he was.

Evander stepped through the door. He was standing tall and composed despite the dust on his boots. He looked so out of place with his polished silver sword at his hip as he stood in the soft light of the bakery. His coat had been brushed clean since last night and he carried himself with a confidence that seemed to draw every eye in the room.

Conversation faltered for moment before resuming as though people couldn't help but notice him but also couldn't quite hold onto the sight. One of the dockworkers dropped his spoon. The sound of it clinking off his mug echoed through the shop. Even the lace curtains seemed to stir as though the air itself bowed toward him.

Morgana ducked her head quickly pretending to wipe a smudge off the glass case. *Of course he's here. Of course.*

"Morning," he said with his voice sounding as smooth and deep as ever.

Her throat felt dry. "We open at seven. You're early." *Why did my voice sound so sharp?*

"It's already half past." His lips curved. It was not quite a smile, but something in between a smile and a slight frown. "I'm right on time."

Tomas bustled forward from the espresso machine ever the friendly host. "New face! What can we do for you sir?"

Evander's eyes didn't leave Morgana. "Cookies."

Morgana stiffened. "We have several kinds. Oatmeal raisin, sugar, ginger spice—"

"Chocolate chip," he interrupted.

Her pulse spiked.

Agnes emerging from the back with a tray of scones, chuckled deeply. "Ah a classic choice. Everyone loves our chocolate chip."

"Yes," Evander said simply. "All of them."

The words hung in the air. Agnes and Tomas exchanged a brief look together and awkwardly chuckled as it was such an unusual request. Morgana's gaze shot to the side shelf where the tin of last night's batch waited like a loaded pistol. Her heart was pounding at the thought of him touching even one of them.

Morgana blinked. "Excuse me?"

"I'll take every chocolate chip cookie you have." His gaze was steady and totally unreadable.

Tomas let out a low whistle. "That's half the jar at least. Planning a party?"

Evander's mouth twitched slightly. "Something like that."

Morgana's fingers tightened around the tongs she held. The cookies. The ones she'd baked this morning carefully *without* magic were ordinary, safe, and wholesome. But the rest of last night's batch the ones touched by her spell had been sealed in the tin on the side shelf. She'd planned to destroy them and grind them down into useless crumbs.

But she hadn't yet.

And now Evander Grimshaw wanted all of them.

"Are you sure?" she asked trying to keep her tone sounding light. "That's well it's a lot of cookies."

"Positive." His eyes met hers steady as a tide. "I've developed a taste for them."

Heat prickled up the back of her neck.

Agnes beamed and bustled to fetch a box. "Wonderful! Morgana would you pack them up dear?"

Of course. Morgana forced a smile and carried the jar behind the counter. Her hands weren't steady. Inside the jar golden-brown rounds gleamed with melted chocolate. They looked as innocent as any pastry. But she knew better. She could feel the faint thrum of the spell still woven through some of them. Her fingertips tingled from the magic as she grabbed them. She was about to hand him some very dangerous items.

He can't take these. Not all of them. The more he eats the stronger it'll bind. I have to—

Her hand hovered over the tin at the side. For a moment she considered palming them away substituting only the safe batch. But Evander's gaze was fixed on her with that unnerving precision as if he'd notice the second she tried to deceive him.

She swallowed and began stacking them into the box.

By the time she closed the lid her palms were damp.

"That'll be six silver," she murmured avoiding his gaze.

Evander pulled out a coin purse and dropped the exact change onto the counter without looking. He lifted the box, nodded his thanks to Agnes and Tomas, then turned back to Morgana.

"See you around."

Her throat bobbed. "Maybe."

The bell jingled as he left.

The moment the door closed behind him Morgana exhaled sharply as she gripped the counter to steady herself.

Tomas chuckled. "That one's got an appetite. Haven't seen a man buy out our whole stock of anything before."

Agnes leaned in conspiratorially. "And handsome too isn't he? Almost makes you wish we were younger eh Morgana?"

Morgana forced a laugh that felt brittle. "Yes. Handsome." *If only they knew the truth. This isn't romance. It's a mistake binding itself tighter with every crumb.*

Her chest felt knotted with tension.

Because even as Evander walked away down the sunlit street she felt it.

A tingling like sparks dancing across her skin. Tiny threads pulling taut in her chest. The air seemed charged and heavy with something unseen.

And it was connected to him.

She pressed her hand against her sternum willing her pulse to slow. She felt like she was about to have a heart attack.

It's the spell. He's carrying it with him. Every bite and every crumb. It's weaving tighter.

She should stop him. She should run after him, take the cookies back, undo what she'd done before it went any further.

But she didn't move.

She couldn't.

Because part of her that was traitorous and reckless wanted to see what would happen. The scent of chocolate lingered thick in the air cloying and heavy as if the spell itself had marked the moment and would not let her forget it.

Chapter 3 – The Spell Takes Hold

The sun had begun to dip behind the rooftops of Eraldor by the time Morgana finally allowed herself a moment of stillness. *The Golden Spoon* was quiet now with the lunch rush long gone and the smell of vanilla and butter lingering on her skin like a gentle memory. She wiped her hands on her apron yet even as she moved toward the back counter to put ingredients away her thoughts were in knots.

It was just a cookie. Just a cookie.

She repeated it like a mantra though she could feel the threads of magic lingering in the air. They felt subtle but insistent, curling around her like invisible vines. If she said it enough maybe she could believe it. Maybe it was possible that the warmth in his eyes and the curve of his smile had nothing to do with her hands or her spell. But the doubt pressed close whispering that she had cheated and stolen a moment that was never meant to be hers. And beneath it all a part of her feared the cruelest truth of all. She wanted him to choose her spell or no spell.

Last night had been a harmless experiment. A pinch of rosehip, a whispered charm, nothing more than a gentle nudge toward warmth and affection.

Except it hadn't been gentle nudge.

Not with Evander Grimshaw.

Her thoughts darted back to him. He was tall, confident, and impossibly composed as he'd carried off every chocolate chip cookie she'd baked. And the way his gaze had lingered on her with that slow deliberate look that had made her stomach flutter in ways she hadn't felt in years.

No. This isn't right.

Her pulse quickened at the memory. She shook her head and turned toward the spice rack hoping the motion would ground her like it usually did. But the tingling sensation returned. It was subtle at first then stronger like a current of energy running beneath her skin.

He's still out there. Carrying it.

Morgana's mind raced. Each step toward the oven felt like wading through fog. She measured flour three times, double-checked the sugar jars, even lined up the muffin tins with obsessive precision, but nothing could distract her from the prickling and almost tangible pull of the magic she had set loose the night before.

And then she saw him.

Evander Grimshaw. He was standing outside the bakery's window framed by the amber glow of the setting sun. He wasn't simply passing by. He was looking in and waiting anxiously. He looked like he belonged in the growing shadows of the evening.

Morgana's breath hitched at the sight of him. *No. This can't be happening.*

Her fingers trembled against the edge of the counter. She pressed her palms to her face trying to steady her heartbeat and convince herself that this was just a coincidence. It was just good timing. But deep down she knew better. The tingling sensation wasn't a trick of her imagination. It was *him*. The spell. The magic had latched onto him and now tugged at her in ways she hadn't anticipated.

By the time he pushed the door open she had attempted to compose herself by smoothing down her apron and forcing a neutral expression.

"Good evening," Evander said casually though the intensity in his gray eyes betrayed him. "I thought I'd see how the bakery looks at sunset."

Morgana blinked slowly. "You're here again?"

"I mentioned I have a taste for your chocolate chip cookies," he said as he stepped inside fully with that same careful grace that somehow made his every movement seem deliberate. "It's an insatiable taste."

Her stomach knotted. *This isn't normal. He shouldn't be here. Not twice in one day. Not just because he likes cookies.*

"Evander..." she started then stopped. Words failed her. *How could she explain that a simple harmless charm had somehow... escalated? That she had unwittingly woven something far stronger than intended?*

He reclined casually against the counter as his gaze locked on hers. "I wanted to see you again too."

Her pulse stuttered. "That's very kind of you."

But kindness alone didn't explain the heat curling in her chest and the way his attention seemed to anchor around her as if some invisible magnet had attached itself to them both.

Oh no.

Evander's presence was magnetic in a way that made Morgana feel as if every sound in the room had dimmed except for his voice and the faint hum of the magic still echoing in her cookies. She could feel it now radiating outward. It was a subtle pressure pressing against her thoughts. It was a pull she couldn't resist no matter how much she willed herself to step away and to treat him as any normal customer.

"More chocolate chip cookies?" she asked hoping to keep her voice steady and to hide the faint tremor that she felt.

He smiled faintly. "I think I'll take a few more if you don't mind."

Her hands froze mid-motion. *He already bought all of them this morning. How is this possible?*

She tried to distract herself by sliding the empty tray aside. "I can bake another batch. It won't take long."

"No need to trouble yourself," he said. His voice sounded low and almost amused. "I wasn't expecting… a special second helping."

And yet his gaze lingered. She felt it everywhere. It felt like it was burning, compelling, and very insistent. Morgana swallowed hard. This was no ordinary infatuation. This was… *the spell.*

She tried to act busy by busying herself with arranging pastries on the shelves and lining up scones and muffins. Her hands shook slightly as she measured powdered sugar and dusted it onto a tray with meticulous care. Her chest constricted. Each thought scattered before she could grasp it. Even her pulse seemed to drum his name.

I didn't mean for it to be like this. I didn't mean this.

Evander moved closer and every step he took sent another ripple through the invisible threads of magic she had woven. It was subtle and almost imperceptible to anyone else but to her it was a storm. It pulled her attention toward him and made her heart race and her stomach twist in ways that left her momentarily breathless.

"I must admit," he said while leaning seductively on the counter, "I can't seem to stay away."

Morgana froze. "Evander…"

"I don't know why," he continued then with his voice low and even, "but something about your… bakery… and you… draws me in."

The words sent a shiver down her spine. She pressed her hand to her chest feeling the fluttering panic as the tingling spread through her limbs. The spell had taken hold far more effectively than she had anticipated. *This isn't attraction. Not normal attraction. This is magic. And it's dangerous.*

She tried to reason with herself as she worked counting cups, measuring ingredients, and rehearsing mundane phrases to distract her mind. But Evander's presence was overwhelming. Every movement he made and every word he said seemed amplified and tugged on the threads she had woven into the cookies.

He's under it. He's really under it. I can feel it.

Her thoughts spiraled. If she didn't act fast the spell could deepen entwining his will with hers more strongly than she intended. And then the responsibility would be hers. The thought made her swallow hard. She had no idea how to undo it safely.

Evander reached for a pastry brushing his fingers against hers as he did so. The contact sent a spark up her arm. Morgana flinched. *No. Stop. This is not normal.*

"You're trembling," he said softly as his gray eyes locked on hers with that unnerving intensity. "Are you... cold?"

"No," she muttered, forcing herself to smile. "I—just... busy."

But her chest tightened as she realized how helpless she felt. The spell wasn't subtle anymore. was very real, very tangible, and it had wrapped around them both like a net. Evander's expression softened yet the pull in her chest made it impossible to think clearly.

I have to fix this. I have to. But how?

The bakery's clock ticked loudly in the silence that had settled between their words. Evander didn't look away. He didn't blink. He simply watched her with every line of his body relaxed yet alert and magnetically drawn. The pull of the magic was almost suffocating. It was a quiet insistence that made her stomach flutter and her thoughts scatter.

"I need to finish preparing the evening batch," she said finally as she retreated toward the kitchen.

He followed at a measured pace never breaking eye contact. "I could help," he offered casually though his tone carried a weight she couldn't ignore.

No. I can't let him touch it. I have to control this before it gets worse.

She shook her head exhaling sharply. "No. It's... complicated."

And it was. Every cookie, every touch, every glance, every subtle motion of his body seemed to send pulses of magic through her. It all anchored him to her and pulled at her awareness demanding a response she couldn't refuse.

I didn't just make cookies. I made a connection. And it's spiraling.

Morgana sank onto a stool behind the counter pressing her hands against her face. Evander stood close by. He was still watching, still drawn, still tethered to her by invisible threads that hummed and thrummed in the air.

And she realized with a cold sinking clarity: she had no idea how to stop it.

Not yet.

Chapter 4 – Rules of Magic

The next morning Morgana arrived at *The Golden Spoon* earlier than usual with her hands trembling slightly as she tied her apron. The bakery greeted her with the mellow perfume of bread just pulled from the oven. She picked up on the smell of warm yeast with a faint edge of the smell of the crisp crust that was still cooling on the trays. Coffee beans had been ground fresh that morning with their bitter nutty aroma cutting through the air like a sharp but steadying hand.

Usually those scents wrapped around her like a comforting quilt. But today even as she wiped down counters and arranged pastries the memory of Evander Grimshaw lingered like a persistent shadow. The memory seemed darker than smoke and just as stubborn.

It's a spell. That's all it is. Just a spell. I can fix this.

She tried to focus on the small tasks in front of her. She focused on folding napkins, polishing the glass cases, and measuring flour. Her hands moved automatically, but her mind raced. She couldn't shake the memory of him standing at the counter last night with his gray eyes fixed on her and the pull of the magic winding tighter around her chest.

It's not attraction. It's the spell. I have to treat it like a tool gone wrong.

She sighed and reached for the sugar jar as if it could provide some tangible comfort.

By mid-morning her friends arrived. Aurelia and Celeste were two women she had grown close to over the years. They stepped into the bakery laughing softly with their voices carrying warmth and familiarity. Morgana managed a small smile though the anxiety coiled tight in her stomach.

"You look like you haven't slept," Aurelia said setting her bag down. "And judging by the look in your eyes it's not just a normal kind of tired."

Morgana bit her lip. "It's... complicated." She gestured vaguely toward the front of the bakery. "Evander came by yesterday. And he took all of the cookies."

Celeste raised a curious eyebrow. "The cookies? You mean the ones you baked the other night?"

"Yes." Morgana's voice dropped to a whisper. "I... I accidentally... added a charm. Just a little one. But..." She faltered her words as she tried not to explain. "...it worked. Too well."

Aurelia and Celeste exchanged a glance the kind of knowing look friends give each other when the situation is about to get messy.

"Wait," Celeste said slowly, "you're telling me you baked chocolate chip cookies with... a love spell in them?"

Morgana's heart thumped. "I didn't mean for it to be anything serious. Just a small nudge. You know a little warmth. Just a little charm to encourage kindness."

"And it backfired," Aurelia supplied while nodding slowly. "I can tell. Just from the way you're pacing and wringing your hands."

"Yes!" Morgana exclaimed as her frustration spilled over. "It's not just him liking the cookies. He's drawn to me. Every time he looks at me it's—" She waved her hands helplessly. "It's stronger than I expected! And I don't know how to undo it!"

Celeste's expression softened. She walked over and rested a hand lightly on Morgana's shoulder. "Morgana… love spells are dangerous. That's why we don't use them casually. They bind feelings in ways that aren't natural and people can't consent to them. If he's under a strong spell like this it's going to be intense."

"I know!" Morgana's voice trembled. "I didn't mean for it to happen. It was supposed to be subtle. Like a whisper in the back of his mind not—" She trailed off feeling overwhelmed.

Aurelia reclined against the counter with her arms folded over chest. "It sounds exactly like a strong love spell potion," she said carefully. "I've read about these kinds of magic. They're tricky because the feelings they create aren't entirely real. Not in the natural sense. And the longer it lingers the harder it is to reverse."

Morgana pressed her palms against her eyes until she saw spots and a low sound escaped from her throat. "I—I should have destroyed the batch. I should have never let him eat the cookies. And now…" She shook her head. "Now he's under it. And I don't know what to do."

Celeste nodded. "Let's figure this out. First you need to understand the rules. Love magic isn't like your everyday enchantments. It can't be turned off once it takes hold at least not easily. The effects grow stronger as the spell interacts with the person's natural emotions. And meddling too much to reverse it can make things… worse."

Morgana sat back staring at the counter. "So... I can't just fix it?"

Celeste shook her head. "Not immediately. Usually the safest way to handle it is to let it naturally run its course. It depends on the strength of the spell. That could take about a week. Sometimes longer. This one seems stronger than most so it might be for longer than usual. During that time you need to be careful with how you interact. Don't encourage it. Don't feed it unintentionally. Just... maintain distance if you can."

Her stomach dropped. "A week? A week of him being like that? Drawn to me? I can't even think about it. What if he notices? What if he does something strange? Or at least strange for someone under the effects of a love spell."

"You'll have to trust yourself," Aurelia said gently. "And trust that the spell will fade on its own. You did this by accident yes, but rushing to undo it can make things worse. Love spells are delicate. Think of them like a wildfire. They are easier to contain if you don't fan the flames and harder if you try to smother it hastily."

After her friends left Morgana sat at the back table of the bakery with a notebook open in front of her. The pages were filled with her messy scrawl. She had spent the better part of the afternoon researching love spells in everything from old magical tomes, modern guides, and even letters from practitioners she'd once apprenticed under. Each source reinforced the same grim reality. Once a strong charm had taken root there was no safe way to immediately reverse it.

It has to run its course... she muttered aloud, tapping a pen against her notebook.

The clock ticked slowly. Morgana's mind refused to rest. She reread passages about magical bonds, charm potency, and ethical guidelines. Some texts mentioned antidotes, but these were mostly warnings about dangerous potions that could backfire or cause lasting harm. The consensus was clear. The magic had to naturally weaken over time. Trying to force a solution risked permanent consequences.

One text caught her attention. It was a leather-bound journal from a practitioner three generations past. The handwriting was cramped and urgent.

Love magic is the most volatile of all enchantments. Unlike charms for warmth or protection, which anchor to physical elements, love magic feeds on emotion itself. Emotions shift like weather. They are sudden, unpredictable, and prone to storms of the heart. A spell cast in tenderness may curdle into obsession. One meant to kindle affection may erupt into all-consuming need. The caster's own feelings bleed into the work and can amplify what was never intended. This is why love magic is forbidden in most circles. Not because it cannot be controlled, but because it refuses to be.

Morgana's hands trembled as she read. The spell she'd cast hadn't been rooted in love. It had been a result of her curiosity, loneliness, and a desire for warmth. But Evander had already occupied her thoughts more than she'd admitted. *Had the spell sensed that? Had it taken what was barely a spark and blown it into wildfire?*

She leaned back as she exhaled slowly though the tension in her shoulders remained. A week. At least a week of watching as Evander Grimshaw's attention was locked on her, of avoiding accidental gestures that might amplify the magic, of pretending that everything was normal when she felt anything but.

I'm not ready for this.

Her fingers drummed against the notebook as she made a list of precautions. Keep interactions minimal. Don't make direct eye contact longer than necessary. Avoid unnecessary conversation. Monitor the strength of the magic. Track his behavior.

She paused realizing the last point was the hardest. *How am I supposed to monitor him without him noticing? Without feeding the spell further?*

A sigh escaped her lips. The thought of a week of controlled interactions and of pretending that everything was ordinary while the magic hummed quietly beneath the surface felt almost impossible. She felt trapped by her own mistake and by her own curiosity and carelessness.

By evening Morgana had tried to focus on the bakery itself. She kneaded dough, measured sugar, and preheated ovens, but the tingling in her chest persisted. It was subtle but constant and a reminder of the consequences of her spell.

She paused to wipe flour from her hands and looked toward the window. The street outside glowed in the warm light of lanterns. A few pedestrians passed by laughing softly and carrying packages from nearby shops. Normal life continued around her. They were oblivious to the magical tension coiling quietly in the bakery.

And she felt a pang of guilt. Evander had done nothing wrong. He had eaten her cookies in good faith and was completely unaware that a charm had taken hold. And now through no fault of his own his thoughts and actions were being influenced by something that wasn't real. Something she had created.

I have to be careful. I can't make this worse.

She opened her notebook again, writing down everything she could remember from the batch. She recorded the precise measurements, the timing, the magical words she had whispered. Each detail was a potential clue and a way to understand the strength and persistence of the spell. Maybe it could help her manage the situation.

But even as she wrote the reality remained clear. There was no immediate fix for this. She could only wait.

A week. Seven days of watching, controlling, and hoping that the magic would fade without causing harm.

Morgana pressed her face into her hands, feeling the weight of responsibility settle heavily on her shoulders. She had always loved magic. She loved its subtle power and its ability to bring warmth or wonder to the world. But this reckless experiment reminded her that magic had rules and boundaries that could not be ignored. And breaking them even unintentionally came at a steep cost.

I'll get through this. I have to.

She lifted her head feeling her determination hardening behind the anxiety. The week ahead would be challenging. Dangerous even. But she wouldn't let the spell ruin her or him.

Not if she could help it.

And with that resolve Morgana turned back to her work. The ovens glowed warmly, the counters gleamed, and the soft scent of pastries filled the air. It was a small comfort. A reminder that even in the chaos of magic there was still order to be found.

Chapter 5 – Awkward Encounters

The morning after her research binge Morgana woke with her cheek pressed to the wooden desk with her hair tangled and the faint imprint of parchment lines pressed into her skin. The candles had burned down to stubby pools of wax leaving the room hazy with the faint scent of smoke. She stretched feeling her bones popping and muttered to herself.

One week. Just one week Morgana Valehart. You can survive anything for seven days.

But the pep talk didn't stop the sick twist in her stomach. A week felt like forever when Evander Grimshaw's gray eyes kept replaying in her mind like a spell she couldn't banish.

The bakery buzzed with its usual morning rhythm. Coffee was brewing, ovens were humming, and the comforting aroma of butter and sugar wrapped around the air like a warm blanket. Morgana tried to lose herself in the air ritual of kneading dough, shaping pastries, and sliding trays into the oven. It almost worked until the bell above the door softly chimed.

Her head snapped up with her heart lurching.

Evander Grimshaw stepped into *The Golden Spoon.*

The man's presence seemed to suck the air from the room. He wasn't particularly loud or flashy, but the spell tugged at her awareness like a string wrapped tight around her ribs. He wore a charcoal-gray coat that fit his broad frame well and his expression was almost unreadable, but his eyes… his eyes found her instantly.

Morgana froze, dough-covered hands suspended midair.

Oh no. Not already.

"Morning," Evander greeted her. His voice sounded deep, steady, and almost casual. But there was something in the way he looked at her as if she were the only person in the room.

"Good morning," Morgana stammered, turning quickly back to her work. Her cheeks heated and she cursed silently. *Composure. Keep your composure.*

He moved to the counter and glanced briefly at the display case though it felt like his attention never really left her. "Do you have any of those cookies left?"

Her stomach dropped. Of course. *The cookies.*

"No," she said too quickly then forced a steadier tone. "I mean not that batch. But we have fresh scones, muffins, cinnamon rolls…" She rattled off the list. The words tumbled out of her mouth like runaway marbles. "The cinnamon rolls are our specialty."

The faintest smile brushed his mouth. It looked almost hesitant as though he'd forgotten the shape of it. "Surprise me then. I trust your judgment more than mine."

The way he said it made her pulse trip over itself. There was trust in his tone as though her opinion mattered more than the menu.

She wiped her floury hands on her apron, grabbed a cinnamon roll, and slid it into a bag. "Here."

Their fingers brushed as she handed it over. Electricity sparked up her arm. It was sharp and undeniable. Evander's gaze sharpened with his breath catching almost imperceptibly.

Morgana jerked her hand back feeling her heart pounding. *Don't feed it. Don't encourage it.*

"That'll be three silver," she said quickly.

He paid, but lingered a moment too long as if he was waiting for her to say something else. When she didn't he gave her one last unreadable look and left. The bell chimed again and the door closed behind him.

Morgana sagged against the counter.

One week. One week.

The next day he came again.

And the next.

By the fourth morning Aurelia had taken notice.

"Your handsome admirer's back," she murmured, leaning toward Morgana as Evander entered the bakery again. Above the bell jingled brightly.

Morgana shot her friend a sharp look. "He's not. Don't say that."

But Aurelia's knowing smirk only widened. Celeste who had been stirring a latte glanced over. "He's been here every day this week. That's not normal bakery behavior or any person under a spell."

It's the spell's affect. Just the spell. Morgana's thoughts screamed the words, but saying them aloud would invite too many questions from nearby customers. Instead she ducked her head and busied herself with the pastry case.

Evander as usual went straight to her. He didn't so much as glance at Aurelia or Celeste. His gray eyes were warm today and almost intent.

"What do you recommend today?" he asked her with his tone low and smooth.

Morgana's hands trembled slightly as she picked up a fresh berry tart and wrapped it. She refused to meet his gaze for too long. "This. It's good. Just finished cooling off."

"Then I'll take it."

Again their hands brushed when she passed him the bag. Again the spark which was stronger this time lit up her nerves. Morgana's pulse stumbled and as a result she felt traitorous warmth climbing her neck.

Morgana forced herself to step back. She stepped back quickly as though distance could smooth the shiver still running through her. She managed a practiced smile though it felt fragile on her lips. "Enjoy your day."

His lips curved faintly in the kind of smile that seemed meant only for her. "I will."

And then he left leaving her rattled.

By the end of the week Morgana's nerves were fraying. Evander's presence filled the bakery daily with his attention always pinned to her. He wasn't pushy and never inappropriate, but there was a steady weight in the way he lingered at the counter and the way his eyes followed her even in silence.

Each time he left she had to grip the counter to steady herself. Her heart hammered as if she'd sprinted a mile.

She tried everything to distance herself. She sent Aurelia or Celeste to the front whenever she could. She hid in the kitchen focusing on dough, batter, and spices. Anything to occupy her. But somehow and some way she always ended up face-to-face with him.

And the worst part? Part of her wanted to be.

On the seventh day she caught herself watching the door before it opened anticipating his arrival.

When Evander finally stepped inside her stomach gave a treacherous flip. He looked tired as though he hadn't slept much, but when his gaze found hers it softened.

She forced herself to look away. *This isn't real. This isn't real.*

Yet as he approached the counter her breath caught.

"Morning," he said. His voice sounded gentler than usual.

"Morning," she echoed wishing her tone didn't sound so small.

He hesitated this time not ordering right away. Instead he studied her with his eyes searching and lingering. "You always look... different here. Lighter. Like the bakery suits you."

Morgana's throat went dry. Compliments were dangerous under the influence of magic. They slipped under defenses too easily burrowing deep.

She forced a shaky laugh. "It's just flour and sugar."

"No," he said simply and firmly as if the thought had never crossed his mind. "It's you."

Her breath hitched. The room seemed to tilt.

Before she could respond Aurelia appeared at her side, sweeping in with practiced ease. "What'll it be today Evander?"

The spell's tension broke like a string snapping and Morgana exhaled shakily grateful for the interruption.

Evander glanced at Aurelia, but his eyes slid back to Morgana almost instantly. "Whatever she recommends."

Morgana wanted to scream. *Stop looking at me like that. It's not you it's me. It's magic.*

Instead she handed him a muffin with trembling fingers. Their hands brushed again, the spark stronger than ever, and she knew with sick certainty that the spell was deepening before it weakened.

Evander accepted the muffin, gave her that quiet lingering look, and then left the bakery.

Morgana collapsed into the nearest chair the moment the door closed.

Celeste raised her brows. "So. Still think this is normal bakery behavior?"

Morgana buried her face in her hands.

"No," she whispered. *Not normal. Not safe. And not going away fast enough.*

Chapter 6 – The Owners' Warning

The bell above the door jingled softly. It was a familiar sound that usually brought comfort to *The Golden Spoon*. But today it felt ominous like a herald of something she wasn't ready to face. Morgana wiped her hands on her apron and tried to steady her nerves. The past week had been exhausting from Evander's constant presence, the spell still lingering, and the weight of knowing she couldn't undo it. It all had left her feeling frayed and jumpy.

She glanced at the counter hoping the owners wouldn't notice her distraction. Agnes and Tomas Fairbairn were the kind elderly couple who owned the bakery. They were seated in their usual chairs behind the front display, sipping tea and observing the bakery with the calm and careful gaze that had kept *The Golden Spoon* running smoothly for decades. Agnes' gray hair was pulled into a neat bun with her eyes twinkling with a gentle warmth while Tomas' mustache twitched slightly as he surveyed the room.

Agnes set down her cup with a soft clink. "Morgana, dear you seem tense this morning. Everything all right?"

Morgana swallowed, forcing a casual smile. "I'm fine, Agnes. Just a busy week."

Tomas nodded slowly. "A busy week indeed. The bakery has been full every day at the same hour. And yet…" His gaze drifted toward the empty counter then back to Morgana. "Something seems… off. A certain energy in the air."

Morgana's stomach twisted. *Energy? Did they feel it too? No it's just intuition. They can't know.*

"I'm sure it's nothing," she said quickly. Her voice sounded a little higher than intended.

Agnes' eyes twinkled faintly. "We both know Morgana that magic isn't always so subtle. You've been here long enough to sense the small ripples in the air."

Morgana froze. The gentle cadence of her words carried a weight that made her chest tighten. The accidental spell was still lingering, pulsing faintly beneath her skin, and she feared that the Fairbairns might sense something without even realizing it.

"I've just been experimenting," she said trying to sound casual. "With… flavors you know. Nothing major."

Tomas leaned forward slightly with his eyes sharp but kind. "Flavors can carry magic if one isn't careful. Remember Morgana our rule has always been clear. No magic in baked goods. It's for the safety of everyone."

Morgana felt her pulse quicken. *They don't know. They have no idea.*

"Yes of course," she said to them while nodding her head quickly. "I understand completely."

Agnes set her cup down again. It was a delicate chime that seemed louder than usual. "We've noticed small anomalies lately. Patrons lingering longer than usual or returning unexpectedly. And the air around the bakery sometimes carries a strange warmth. It feels very subtle but persistent."

Morgana's heart hammered. *They've noticed the effects of the spell without knowing why. How much do they sense?*

"I... I thought it might just be the new recipes," she said, keeping her voice steady. "You know different flavors and some seasonal specials."

Tomas arched an eyebrow. "Perhaps. But unusual coincidences tend to repeat themselves don't they? We've been running this bakery for decades and I don't recall such patterns before."

"We've seen it before dear. A bakery ruined because the bread carried spells instead of yeast. The townsfolk don't forgive easily when their will is tampered with. That's why our rule exists." Agnes looked at her with a mixture of care and warning.

Morgana's hands itched to smooth her apron out and to ground herself in the basic action. Every muscle in her body wanted to run, hide, undo the magic, erase the week. *Just a week and it's already out of control.*

Agnes' gaze softened though her tone remained gentle yet firm. "Morgana you are talented, clever, and we trust you. But magic is a powerful thing. Even small unintentional spells can ripple outward in unexpected ways. That's why the rule exists."

Morgana swallowed hard feeling the weight of their words. She wanted to tell them everything and to confess her mistake, but the fear of consequence, of being dismissed, of harming Evander, and of violating their trust stopped her.

"Yes I know," she murmured barely audible. "I'll be careful." *Little do they know though.*

Tomas nodded seemingly satisfied. "Good. We know you will. Just remember that sometimes restraint is the greater talent Morgana. Your skill is evident in every tray, every loaf, every cookie. Don't let experimentation overshadow caution."

Morgana felt a shiver run down her spine. Their words were meant to be supportive, but they carried the weight of warning. Every glance, every tone, every subtle shift of expression reminded her of the delicate balance she had disrupted.

I've broken the balance. And now I have to survive the consequences until the spell fades.

As the day progressed Morgana moved through the bakery with heightened awareness. Every chime of the door made her flinch. Every step of a customer felt exaggerated as though she could sense the faint pull of her magic on everyone around her.

Evander arrived as he had every day this week. His gray eyes found her immediately. They carried that pull she couldn't resist. She forced herself to look down and to busy herself with arranging muffins and croissants yet every instinct screamed at her. *Don't engage. Don't feed it.*

Aurelia noticing Morgana's tension approached with a knowing glance. "He's here again," whispered to her while leaning closer.

Morgana nodded at her and could feel her heart hammering. "I know. I... I just..." She bit her lip trying to steady her voice. "I don't want to make it worse."

Celeste appeared beside her and placed a comforting hand on her shoulder. "You've been careful though. That's what matters. Just... keep your focus Morgana. Don't let the spell dictate your actions."

Morgana exhaled as she shook her head slightly. "I thought I could manage it. I thought I could keep it under control."

"But it's magic," Aurelia said softly. "Magic rarely stays under control once it's been released. You've already felt its pull haven't you?"

Morgana's fingers clenched around a tray of scones. "Every single day."

She politely talked to Evander not wanting to appear rude to a customer. The Fairbains would be very angry at her for that slight. "Can I interest you in a fresh baked muffin? Just out of the oven and still warm."

He looked both delighted and relieved at her taking with him. "Any recommendations from you are welcome."

As she puts a blueberry muffin on a plate for him her hands slightly shook. Of course Evander immediately noticed that. "Something wrong?"

Morgana blushed strongly. She quietly admitted to him. "I… may have misjudged a spell earlier this week. Nothing dangerous! Just… messier than I meant."

Later when the bakery quieted for a moment in the early afternoon lull Tomas approached her at the counter. "Morgana may I speak with you privately for a moment?"

She nodded at him and then walked to the small office at the back. The air inside was still and the faint scent of vanilla lingered in the air.

"You've been working diligently and we are proud of your skill," he began with his voice sounding gentle. "But we've noticed some subtle changes lately. Patrons returning at unusual times with behaviors that seem… influenced. And the air…there's a warmth we cannot attribute to the ovens alone."

Morgana's stomach twisted. *They've felt it. They've sensed the effects of the spell... but they don't know what caused it.*

"I... I'm not sure what you mean," she said carefully, forcing a neutral tone.

Tomas gave her a patient look. "I do not mean to accuse or chastise. We only ask that you remember the rule. No magic in baked goods. It exists to protect everyone including the customers, the staff, even the baker herself."

Morgana swallowed hard. "Of course. I... I'll remember."

"Good," he said with a nod then placed a hand on her shoulder. "You're talented Morgana. That is why we trust you. But talent without care can become dangerous. Even the smallest spell can have consequences beyond our sight."

Her pulse quickened with a mixture of fear and guilt twisting in her stomach. "Yes I understand."

As Tomas left the room Morgana sank into a chair. She pressed her hands to her face. Her thoughts raced. *They have no idea it's him. Evander. I can't let them know. I can't...*

The accidental spell had set off a chain reaction she couldn't control. The Fairbairns' subtle warnings only reminded her of the fragility of the situation. She was treading a dangerous line between maintaining the bakery's rules, keeping Evander safe from manipulation, and trying not to unravel herself entirely.

The rest of the day passed in a blur. Every interaction, every glance, every fleeting brush of fingers became a source of panic. Evander arrived in his usual quiet and steady way completely unaware of the chaos his presence caused. He smiled, took his order, and lingered just enough to pull at her awareness. It was just enough to remind her of the power of the spell she had unleashed.

Morgana moved mechanically preparing trays, serving pastries, and keeping her distance all while her mind raced for ways to maintain control. She glanced toward the front where Agnes and Tomas quietly observed. Their expressions were a mixture of concern and gentle authority. She dared not let her panic show.

One misstep, one accidental flicker of magic, and they'll know. And then...

She exhaled slowly. The week of consequences stretched endlessly before her, but for now she had to focus on maintaining composure, following the rules, and keeping the spell in check.

Because breaking the rule had consequences. They seemed small at first, but they were growing steadily. And Morgana Valehart was starting to feel the weight of every single one.

Chapter 7 – The First Misstep

The night was still. It was the kind of quiet that pressed against the windows of *The Golden Spoon* and made every creak and whisper of the rafters feel amplified. Morgana Valehart sat perched on a stool in the kitchen, her apron dusted with flour, and her hands clenched around a mug of cooling chamomile tea. The spell she had cast that morning had gone horribly irreversibly wrong. She had meant only to add a whisper of sweetness and luck to a batch of cinnamon buns.

It had started as a simple charm. It was a gentle enhancement to a familiar recipe. Morgana had carefully murmured the incantation picturing the warmth of sunlight in every roll of dough. And for a moment it had felt perfect. But then the dough had shimmered unnaturally, too brightly, and a faint hum had filled the kitchen vibrating in her bones. Panic had taken hold instantly. *What have I done?* she thought, with her heart hammering hard. She tried to nullify the spell and to retract it before anyone noticed, but her trembling hands had only amplified the magic.

Now hours later she could still feel it pulsing. It felt like a quiet insistent heartbeat in the air around her. Flour floated faintly suspended like mist in the light of the lantern and the scent of cinnamon had become almost sharp and overpowering. She pressed her palms to her face hoping to will it away, but even that had seemed to make the magical residue cling more stubbornly.

And then there was Evander. She couldn't escape thinking of him. It was as if the universe had conspired to tether him to her panic. The young man had stopped by that morning to pick up a batch of pastries and Morgana could swear he had noticed something. His grey eyes had lingered too long, flicking over her flushed face and the stray tendrils of hair that clung to her temples. Every small blush and awkward glance felt magnified like the spell itself had made her hyper-aware of him.

The real mischief however came in a form she had not anticipated at all. Sprinkles.

It started with a single batch of cupcakes. Morgana had sprinkled them with the usual rainbow topping intending only to make them visually appealing. But when she looked again a faint shimmer ran across the sugary surface and the sprinkles seemed to rearrange themselves into letters. "You've got this, Morgana!" it read.

She blinked in complete disbelief. Slowly she leaned closer and wondered if her eyes were playing tricks. The sprinkles shifted again forming a new message: "Evander likes your cinnamon buns."

Morgana yelped at seeing that. She stumbled back and narrowly avoided knocking over a container of flour. Her heart raced. It was half with panic and half with incredulous amusement. *Even the sprinkles are conspiring against me,* she muttered under her breath while wishing fervently that the Fairbairns were not in the other room.

By the end of the day it had become a running series of messages. Sometimes they were encouragements for her like "Breathe you're amazing!" or "Smile at him it's cute!" Other times they were teasing her almost like a mischievous wingman "Blushes suit you." Morgana tried desperately to maintain her composure by shaking her head and pretending the sprinkles were behaving normally whenever the elderly owners wandered by.

"Everything alright here?" Agnes asked one time as her gentle eyes caught Morgana mid-stifled giggle.

Morgana froze with her fingers dusted with powder sugar. "Yes! Just… cleaning," she said to the woman though her voice sounded a little too high-pitched even to her. She quickly swept the cupcakes behind her apron hoping the messages wouldn't be visible.

Tomas chuckled softly. "You do seem… animated."

Morgana offered a strained smile and muttered something about long hours. As soon as they left she crouched beside the counter and whispered, "Okay sprinkles keep it down! The owners can't know." But the sprinkles clearly enjoying themselves shifted into another message: "You're adorable when flustered. Evander notices."

Her cheeks warmed and she had to bite her lip to stop herself from laughing. It was utterly impossible to maintain her usual professional demeanor with the tiny sugar allies cheering her on in such a mischievous way. And yet there was a feeling of comfort in it. Amid the chaos of her misfired spell, the sleepless nights, and the pounding of her heart at every glance from Evander she felt kinda supported.

When Evander returned the following day the cupcakes had gathered a faint shimmer of magic still lingering in the sprinkles. Morgana set them on the counter carefully, praying that nothing overt appeared. Evander's eyes flicked over the treats.

"They look… perfect," he said while raising an eyebrow. "Even better than usual."

Morgana's stomach fluttered. "Tank you," she stammered out and then pressed a hand to her cheek as if it might disguise the blush spreading across it. She kept a casual eye on the cupcakes worried the messages would reveal themselves. The sprinkles however remained oddly still this time as if they knew an audience was present.

After a brief bite where he seemed to savor the taste Evander smiled at her. "They taste even better too."

"I'm a bit surprised. Let's just say magic and I aren't always on the same page."

"Well apparently it works out sometimes."

After he left Morgana slumped against the counter and let out a long breath. "Alright little sprinkles," she said sternly to them, "I need you to behave until I fix this spell. I mean it." The sprinkles who ignored her entirely immediately shifted to form a new message: "Even magic agrees: blush more around him."

Morgana groaned and then buried her face in her hands. The absurdity of it all from sitting in her bakery at midnight and talking to enchanted sprinkles that were apparently her romantic cheerleaders made her feel both panicked and inexplicably giddy. She snorted quietly to herself. *How did my life come to this?*

Despite the chaos the sprinkles became a subtle comfort. Each message reminded her that she was not entirely alone in her mishap and that perhaps the universe or at least a cheeky portion of her magic was rooting for her. They pushed her gently, encouraged her with Evander, and even taught her to laugh at herself just a little.

Still hiding the messages from Agnes and Tomas remained a high-wire act. Morgana devised creative methods for it. She did it by subtly tilting trays, dusting the cupcakes lightly to obscure words, or distracting the owners with questions about orders.

Sometimes she imagined them noticing and shaking their heads at her antics but thankfully it never came to that.

By the third day Morgana had begun to anticipate the messages as if the sprinkles themselves were reading her mind. "You're stronger than you think," appeared when she doubted herself mid-spell. "Go talk to him," flashed when she lingered too long in thought about Evander. She started to consider them allies in more ways than one. They were like tiny sugar assistants guiding her through both magic and matters of the heart.

And yet the misstep that had started it all remained unresolved. Morgana still spent sleepless nights testing, chanting, and cautiously observing the magical tremors in the bakery. But now with the sprinkles offering encouragement and subtle nudges she felt a little braver. She could face the challenge and perhaps face Evander too without completely unraveling.

That evening she whispered to the sprinkles as she arranged cupcakes on a tray: "Alright team one last push. Let's fix this spell together and maybe just maybe… let's not scare him off in the process okay?"

The sprinkles responded immediately forming a bright little message: "We believe in you. Go get him Chef Morgana."

Morgana laughed quietly, hiding behind the counter to conceal her flushed face. The tiny magical allies had become her secret support system. They were a reminder that even in moments of panic and error there could be joy, humor, and hope.

And so the misstep that had begun with a flawed spell had become something entirely unexpected. It became a series of quiet and glittering messages, encouragement from her own magic, and the soft insistent awareness that Evander's presence though nerve-wracking was now something she could not help but treasure.

Chapter 8 – Unintended Consequences

The morning light filtered into *The Golden Spoon* like liquid gold, and spilling across the counters and warming the air already sweet with the scent of fresh-baked honey cakes. Morgana Valehart stood at the long wooden table in the kitchen with her sleeves rolled up to her elbows and her hair escaping from its braid. The oven hummed steadily, filling the space with the comfortable rhythm of a bakery at work.

She should have felt at ease mornings were her sanctuary after all and they were the hours before the doors opened when she could lose herself in kneading dough and stirring sugar. But today her nerves prickled like static. She felt restless and uncomfortable.

The sprinkles had behaved overnight with no messages scrawled across the counter or into the tops of her cupcakes. And yet the thought of them and the lingering residue of her miscast spell clung to her like a second skin. She had not yet been able to undo it at least not completely yet. Which meant every interaction she had with Evander carried the dangerous possibility that his reactions were not wholly his own.

Her stomach flipped when the bell over the bakery door chimed. She didn't need to peek out front to know who it was.

Evander Grimshaw.

His footsteps were unhurried and confident as he crossed the tiled floor to the counter. Morgana turned quickly, dusting flour from her hands onto her apron, and forcing a smile she wasn't sure reached her eyes.

"Morning," he said. His voice was as rich and warm as it ever sounded. He leaned against the counter in his usual relaxed way though today his gaze seemed to linger longer than usual. It kept sweeping from her face to her flour-streaked limbs and then back again.

"Morning," Morgana replied grateful her voice came out steady. She busied herself arranging scones on a tray. Anything to keep her hands moving and her thoughts from spiraling.

Evander chuckled softly. "You work too hard. Anyone ever tell you that?"

She shot him a glance caught off guard by the fondness in his tone. "I like to keep busy," she said quickly.

This time he didn't just let the conversation drift. Instead he reached across the counter with his hand brushing hers as he picked up one of the scones. The touch was light and almost accidental, but her entire body jolted as though he'd pressed a brand into her skin.

Morgana's breath caught.

She snatched her hand back feeling heat blooming in her cheeks. "Careful they're still hot," she said the words tumbling out clumsily.

Evander unfazed smiled faintly. "So are you."

Her heart stumbled over itself. *That's not normal,* she thought frantically. *He wouldn't say something like that. Not to me. Not unless...*

Unless the spell.

Guilt wrapped itself around her like ivy creeping higher with each passing moment. *Was this real? Was Evander actually choosing to be more familiar or was it just the lingering residue of her misstep coaxing him closer?* The thought made her want to both lean into his warmth and run from it entirely.

Throughout the day the little gestures continued. When she carried trays from the kitchen to the front he reached to steady her with his hand brushing the small of her back. When she passed him a tart their fingers touched again. It felt like it was done too deliberately and too long for it to be accidental. And as always his eyes found hers warm and searching as though he could see straight through her flustered attempts at composure.

By noon Morgana's thoughts were a tangled mess.

She caught her reflection in the polished copper pot hanging above the stove. Her cheeks were pink, her lips pressed tight, and her eyes darting nervously. Seeing that she scolded herself. *You should tell him. You should confess that the spell is to blame and that he might be under its influence. It isn't fair to let this happen.*

And yet the words refused to leave her lips. Each time he smiled at her and each time his hand brushed hers something in her chest ached in a way she could not bear to end.

The Fairbairns bustled in and out during the afternoon rush too distracted by customers to notice the strange atmosphere. Morgana clung to that luck like a lifeline, praying they wouldn't pick up on the obvious tension sparking between her and Evander.

It was near closing time when the real test came. Morgana was wiping down the counter lost in thought when Evander reached out and gently caught her wrist. She froze still with the rag slipping from her hand.

"Morgana," he said softly.

Her name on his lips felt different today. It seemed heavier somehow. She swallowed hard with her pulse thundering in her ears. "Yes?"

His thumb brushed lightly across the inside of her wrist before he seemed to realize what he was doing. His gaze locked onto hers. It was steady and searching and she felt herself drowning in it.

For a heartbeat the bakery was silent and the world narrowed to only him and the impossible warmth blooming in her chest.

She pulled her hand back gently with her heart twisting painfully. "I—I should finish cleaning," she stammered as she retreated into the safety of movement.

The look that flickered across his face stabbed at her. It was full of confusion and maybe a hint of hurt. But she couldn't, *wouldn't*, let herself believe it was genuine.

Because if it wasn't real and if it was only the spell then she was stealing something from him.

That night sleep refused her again. She lay on her narrow cot, staring at the ceiling as shadows shifted across the beams. Her thoughts circled endlessly like a carousel she couldn't step off.

What if it's the spell? What if every touch and every look isn't really him? What if I'm the thief of his sincerity?

Her chest ached with longing, with guilt, and with the unbearable question of what if.

She thought of his hand against hers and of the warmth that lingered even after he let go. She pressed her palm to her chest willing her heartbeat to calm, but it only beat faster.

The bakery felt different the next morning. It felt charged as though the very walls hummed with her secret. She worked in silence feeling too jittery to hum the little tunes she usually did. Even the sprinkles on the counter seemed subdued. They offered no mischievous encouragement today.

Evander arrived later than usual and when he stepped inside the air thickened instantly. He greeted her with a smile softer than sunlight, but Morgana couldn't return it fully. She busied herself with the bread loaves. She arranged them and rearranged them until it was almost comical.

"Are you avoiding me?" he asked finally his tone was light but his gaze was sharp.

Morgana stiffened. "Of course not."

He stepped closer to her. It was close enough that she could feel the warmth radiating from him. "Good. Because I'd hate to think I'd done something wrong."

Her throat constricted. *It isn't you. It's me. It's the spell.*

But the words wouldn't come.

Instead she muttered something about busy mornings and slipped past him into the kitchen clutching at the cool handle of a mixing bowl like it might anchor her to reality.

Behind her Evander chuckled softly. It wasn't mocking nor frustrated, but just amused and impossibly fond.

Something sharp lodged beneath her ribs making it hard to take a deep breath.

That evening when the bakery was finally quiet and the Fairbairns had gone upstairs Morgana leaned heavily against the counter while she stared at the cooling racks lined with pastries. Her hands trembled slightly and her chest ached with guilt.

"This isn't right," she whispered into the silence. "Not until I fix it. Not until I know."

The sprinkles shimmered faintly on a stray cupcake left behind spelling out only two words: "Trust him."

Morgana pressed her hands to her burning cheeks feeling torn between laughter and despair.

If only it were that simple.

Chapter 9 – Public Mishaps

The Golden Spoon had always been a stage for whispers. They were usually the kind that fluttered from table to table like the crumbs Morgana swept up at the end of every shift. People here came for the bread yes, but they stayed for the chatter: who was getting married, whose son had left for the capital, and which harvest had failed or flourished. Morgana had grown used to their hum safe in her corner behind the counter. She was often shielded by sugar, butter, and the rhythm of kneading dough.

But lately the whispering had shifted and more often than not she found the threads of it tangled around her name.

It began subtly. A laugh too loud when Evander leaned closer than necessary to point at her tray of fruit tarts. A knowing look when his hand brushed hers as she passed him a basket of rolls. A perceptive smile from Agnes who had always loved her stories but now seemed to enjoy watching her squirm even more.

Morgana tried to ignore it. Tried to remind herself that the miscast enchantment that had bound her to Evander in ways she still didn't fully understand was to blame. His sudden gentleness and the way he lingered in her space as if tethered wasn't natural. It wasn't him. It wasn't real.

And yet…

When Evander leaned across the counter one bright morning and slid a coin toward her with the deliberate slowness of a man who wanted her to notice his hand she could feel something like butterflies in her chest. His eyes caught hers and held. "Careful," he said with his voice low. "You've powdered your cheek with flour again."

Morgana's hand flew to her face feeling heat rushing up her neck. Oh no, oh no, oh no. "Oh! Well thank you I suppose." She fumbled for a rag and ducked away before he could see her expression.

Behind them two of the shop's oldest regulars the Townsend sisters exchanged a glance that spoke volumes.

"Did you hear that?" whispered Lillian to her sister with her sharp nose twitching as though she'd sniffed out a scandal.

"I did," said Maribelle as her voice lilted with amusement. "And did you see the way he looked at her?"

Morgana's stomach sank as she overheard them. *Wonderful. Just wonderful. Next they'll be writing ballads about us and handing them out with the croissants.*

The days that followed only worsened matters.

Evander had always been attentive in his own way. He was serious, watchful, and steady as a stone. But now? He seemed unable to stop finding reasons to linger near her. A hand hovering just behind her elbow when she bent to retrieve a tray. His thumb brushing against her wrist as he accepted his change. A low chuckle at jokes she hadn't meant as particularly funny.

At first Morgana assumed it was just her imagination maybe her guilty conscience weaving fancies out of coincidence. *It's all in your head. He's just polite. You're overreacting.*

But the customers noticed. Oh did they notice.

"Looks like you've found yourself a shadow," said Old Man Greaves one afternoon as he peered over his spectacles as Evander stood unusually close by the shelves of rye bread.

"A loyal shadow at that," Agnes added knowingly. She was smiling as she slid a tray of muffins into the display.

Morgana forced a laugh. "He just… likes bread," she muttered while praying the conversation would die there. *Please for the love of sugar and sanity let it die there.*

It didn't.

Soon the bakery became a theater for speculation. Whenever Evander walked through the door all eyes turned waiting for the next display of attentiveness. And when it inevitably came in the form of his fingers brushing a loose strand of hair from Morgana's face or his hand steadying hers when she lifted a tray too heavy the murmurs rose like a tide.

"Such a gentleman."

"Don't they look sweet together?"

"About time she found someone who notices her."

Morgana wished the floorboards would open beneath her. *I should've studied counter-spells harder. One misstep and now half the town thinks I'm starring in some romantic farce.*

The worst came on market day.

The bakery was packed and the air thick with the scent of cinnamon and butter. Morgana was juggling orders with her hands moving faster than she ever thought possible when Evander appeared at her side. Without a word he reached over the counter to adjust her apron strap which had slipped loose. His fingers lingered on her shoulder. They felt warm, steady, intentional.

The room went silent.

Every customer in the shop seemed to pause as their gazes swung conspiratorially toward the pair of them like weather vanes in a sudden wind. Morgana's breath caught. *Not here. Not in front of everyone. Please Evander don't—*

"Uh—thank you," she stammered as she tugged the strap herself desperate to break the contact.

"You're welcome," Evander said. His tone was gentle enough to make her heart trip.

The silence broke into a chorus of whispers.

"That was—did you see—"

"Clear as day!"

"I'll wager they're courting mark my words."

Morgana's ears burned. She ducked her head, fumbling with the cash drawer as if its clinking coins might drown out the commentary. But the words followed her. They were sticky and relentless and all she could think was: *They can't know. They mustn't know.*

Aurelia being ever helpful around the bakery was wiping down a work table back in the kitchen. Morgana was grateful for her help and constant companionship. She lowered her voice so only Morgana could hear. "You know what this reminds me of? Bellrose's bakery. Fifty years ago she spelled her bread to keep customers coming back. At first no one noticed, but soon people realized they didn't want anything else. They weren't choosing anymore. And once choice was gone so was trust. The bakery didn't last a season after that."

Morgana blanched at hearing the comparison. Everyone knew the story and the ramifications. Magic users all over the city were cautious because of the tale and the negative impact of it. *If the Fairbains or the general public were to find out I would be ruined.*

The bell over the door jingled again just as the whispers began to ebb and in tumbled the Whitcombe children. The three of them were red-cheeked from running through the market square. Their mother trailed behind with a weary smile already apologizing for their noise.

The children swarmed the counter like sparrows as they pointed at buns, tarts, and the tall tower of sugared biscuits Morgana had arranged only an hour ago.

"I want the big one!" cried Timothy the eldest.

"No I want it!" Clara countered tugging on his sleeve.

The littlest Rosie pressed her nose to the glass and squealed, "Look Mama sprinkles!"

Morgana leaned down softening her tone. "One at a time little dears. Everyone will get a treat."

Evander appeared then carrying a tray of cooled loaves from the back as though the bakery had always been his to help in. He set them down near Morgana close enough that his arm brushed hers and close enough that the Whitcombe children noticed immediately.

Clara gasped while clutching her brother's sleeve. "Mama, Mama—look! He touched her arm!"

Timothy squinted with his expression caught between suspicion and delight. "Is he her sweetheart?"

The words rang through the bakery like a bell. A couple of customers chuckled into their cups. Agnes's lips twitched as though she were swallowing a grin.

Morgana froze, her face blazing. *Please no, not this, not from children of all people.*

Rosie piped up bouncing on her toes. "He looks at her like Papa looks at you Mama!"

Their poor mother turned beet red and hurried to shush them down while stammering apologies. But the children were not done.

"Does he give her kisses when no one's watching?" Clara asked with unholy glee.

Timothy added sagely, "If he does I bet it's gross."

The bakery erupted with laughter with even Old Man Greaves chuckling into his teacup. Morgana wanted nothing more than to crawl inside the oven and slam the door behind her.

Evander meanwhile only looked faintly amused with the corner of his mouth tugging upward as though he'd found the whole thing charming. He leaned just close enough that only Morgana could hear and murmured, "Should I deny it or let them win their guesses?"

Her stomach swooped. *Don't you dare play along. Don't you dare encourage this spell's mess!* She shot him a glare sharp enough to curdle milk though it was ruined by the furious pink staining her cheeks.

"Children say the strangest things," Morgana said loudly, forcing a laugh as she handed over the bag of sugared biscuits. "Don't they?"

But the damage was done. Every eye in the bakery glittered with delight and the whispers already weaving into tomorrow's gossip.

I can't let this keep spiraling. If even children are noticing it's only a matter of time before someone puts the pieces together.

After the commotion Morgana quietly asked Evander if she could talk privately with him for a moment.

He immediately nodded and replied "Of course."

She gently pulled him aside into the small office. "I think you should know. This isn't your fault. It's... mine. I messed up a spell and it didn't quite fade the way I thought it would."

"You have nothing to worry about. Don't worry!" He chuckled at her overt worry. He was both amused and touched with her being so concerned.

That night Morgana couldn't sleep.

She lay in her narrow bed staring at the ceiling beams with her heart thudding with every remembered touch and every murmur of speculation. Her magic had twisted something natural into something dangerous. It wasn't just her secret anymore. It was bleeding into the lives of others and into the very community she'd tried so hard to belong to.

And worse a part of her that was entirely traitorous and selfish didn't want it to stop.

Because when Evander looked at her with that softness in his eyes she could almost believe it wasn't the spell. *Almost believe that somewhere beneath the enchantment is a man who might have chosen me anyway.*

Her chest ached with the weight of it.

She sat up pressing her palms to her eyes. *No. I can't let it continue. The whispers are already circling like crows. If I don't find a way to reverse the spell or at least muffle its effects then everything will unravel. I'll lose the bakery. I'll lose Agnes and Tomas. I'll lose the fragile safety I've carved out of flour and sugar.*

And Evander would lose the chance to choose freely.

The thought burned worse than any shame. *I can't take that from him. Not him.*

The next morning Morgana resolved to act.

She moved through her baking with new determination. Every knead and fold and whisk was a silent promise: *I will fix this. Even if it breaks my heart to do it.*

Chapter 10 – Friends' Intervention

The parchment was small enough to tuck inside her apron pocket, but Morgana's hand trembled as she wrote. Each loop of ink felt heavier than the last as though the words themselves carried the weight of her secret.

Please. Meet me after close. Urgent.

She hesitated then signed it simply with an "M." Aurelia and Celeste would know. They always knew when her nerves were stretched thin and when she smiled too brightly to hide frayed edges.

She folded the note quickly and slipped it into Aurelia's basket of dried herbs when she stopped by for her evening purchase. Celeste's copy was tucked beneath the ribbon of her order of honey cakes. It was hidden beneath layers of parchment so no curious eye could find it.

By the time *The Golden Spoon's* shutters were drawn and the warm lamplight inside dimmed Morgana's nerves had knotted so tightly she could hardly breathe. Evander had been there earlier of course. And today he'd lingered far too long at the counter with his fingers brushing hers when he accepted his change. His gaze had softened. It was almost tender looking as though there was more behind it than polite courtesy.

If this is him and if this is real then I've cursed myself in more ways than one. And if it isn't real… then I've stolen the choice away from him.

The guilt twisted deeper in her stomach than hunger pangs.

She heard the knock at the back door just as she was finishing scrubbing down the counters for the night. Soft and patterned. Two then three knocks. Their signal.

Morgana opened it to find Aurelia already frowning with her braid half-undone as though she'd rushed here without caring how she looked. Celeste on the other hand strolled in behind her carrying a basket of candied nuts and looking far too pleased with herself.

"Well," Celeste said while hopping up onto the nearest stool as if she owned the place, "someone's in trouble. And by the look on your face it's worse than running out of cinnamon again."

"Sit," Aurelia said briskly as she tugged off her gloves. "Tell us everything before you burst."

Morgana did. She told them about the spell, about her attempt to nullify it, about the way Evander's eyes now lingered and how even the sprinkles had joined the conspiracy of embarrassing her.

Celeste's laughter broke like sunlight through storm clouds. "Sprinkles spelling messages? Saints preserve us Morgana your own sweets are matchmaking! Please tell me they at least spelled something romantic not just 'kiss him, you coward.'"

Morgana buried her face in her hands. "It was worse! They spelled out nice hands right after Evander took a tray from me. He looked so confused and I had to sweep the counter clean before Tomas saw."

Celeste cackled, nearly falling off the stool. Aurelia however only pressed her lips together clearly fighting not to smile.

"This isn't funny," Morgana said with her voice muffled by her palms. "I don't know what's real anymore. If Evander looks at

71

me like that because of me or because of some blasted ripple of magic I can't control. And if the Fairbairns notice…" She trailed off. She could feel the dread coiling sharp and heavy in her stomach.

Aurelia reached across the counter, prying Morgana's hands away from her face with gentle insistence. "Listen to me. Spells don't anchor themselves in hearts without a tether. If there's an effect still weaving around him it's weaker than before. Which means one of two things: either his feelings are growing alongside it or he already had seeds of affection that the magic watered. Either way it isn't wholly fabricated."

Seeds of affection? From Evander? Before all this?

Her pulse stuttered. Hope warred with shame.

Celeste chimed in. She leaned her chin into her palm. "And let's be honest darling the man watches you like you're the last loaf of bread in Eraldor. Spell or no spell."

"Celeste," Aurelia warned.

"What?" Celeste spread her hands. "You wanted her to feel better didn't you?"

Morgana wanted to laugh and cry all at once. Relief pricked her eyes with warmth, but frustration pressed close behind it. "So what do I do? I can't risk him being under even a trace of magic's sway. It isn't fair to him."

Aurelia nodded solemnly. "There are ways to weaken lingering enchantments. Infuse counters with your own intent, but gentler. More like unwinding a knot instead of cutting it. I can show you the herbs that help dilute excess power. Lavender, chamomile, rosemary. Brew them into teas or weave them into your workspace. Let the spell unravel slowly so his will fills the space instead."

Morgana swallowed hard. "And if that means he... stops looking at me that way?"

"Then you'll know the truth," Aurelia said. "And that's better than doubting every glance."

Celeste kicked her heels against the stool smirking. "And if he keeps looking at you like that well... then maybe it's time you stopped hiding behind counters and sprinkles hm?"

Heat climbed Morgana's neck and ultimately pooling at the tips of her ears. *Confess? As if I could. Imagine telling him: oh by the way I might have accidentally enchanted your heart when I was trying to make better food.*

Her laugh was torn between nerves and exhaustion.

Aurelia clapped her hands together. "Enough whining. We have work to do." She pulled a small basket from her cloak. The basket was lined with tiny bundles of herbs and a candle in soft violet wax. "This is simple but effective. We'll start here. Chamomile to soothe lingering threads, lavender to cleanse intent, rosemary to protect the heart of the spell."

Morgana leaned over with her eyes wide. *It's beautiful, but also terrifying. I have to do this right or everything collapses.*

"First you'll brew a small tea of chamomile and rosemary," Aurelia instructed. Her fingers were deft as she tied the bundles with thread. "Sip a little bit and then inhale the steam while focusing on untangling the spell. Picture it loosening. Then light the candle. Place it near your workspace and let the lavender scatter on the counter. The key is to imagine Evander's true feelings filling the space gently and not forcing them."

Morgana nodded trembling. *This is delicate. One wrong thought...* She took the herbs with her fingers brushing Aurelia's and she felt an odd steadiness settle over her. *I'm not entirely alone in this.*

Celeste clapped her hands together nearly knocking over the tea pot. "While you're brewing let's do some practice confessions! Nothing says 'I'm not embarrassed' like rehearsing ridiculous and impossible things."

Morgana groaned. "Celeste I do not—"

"Oh come now," Celeste interrupted her and waving a finger. "Say it like this: 'Evander I must confess I may have enchanted you slightly while trying to make the perfect baked goods and also your hands are nice.' Go on say it!"

Morgana buried her face in her hands again, muffling a laugh. *I cannot say that. Ever. Not in a million years.*

Aurelia shot Celeste a pointed look, but couldn't hide the corner of her smile. "She doesn't have to say it aloud. Visualization counts too. Imagine the words floating gently into the air for your own clarity."

Morgana's shoulders slumped slightly. *Visualization. I can do that. That I can manage.* She pictured herself standing in the empty bakery telling Evander the truth softly with honesty and care. No magic and no sprinkles. Just the truth.

Celeste who was still grinning leaned back. "See? Even without actual words you're practicing bravery. Tiny steps darling. Also if this works I expect cookies as a reward. Preferably cinnamon."

Morgana chuckled despite herself. It was the first genuine smile in days. Relief coiled softly in her chest mingling with the anxiety she couldn't quite shake. *I have allies. I have support. I am not alone.*

They worked late into the evening. Aurelia guided her hands through arranging the herbs, lighting the candle, and focusing her intent. Morgana followed each step meticulously. She inhaled the chamomile and rosemary steam while imagining the threads of the spell gently untangling. Celeste hovered nearby, narrating wildly improbable scenarios to keep the mood light such as Evander bursting into a waltz in the bakery or sprinkles forming a banner over his head reading "I like Morgana."

Morgana laughed more than she had in weeks feeling the tension inside her loosening fractionally. *I can't control everything, but I can act. I can try. That has to count for something.*

When the ritual was complete Aurelia examined the candles and herbs nodding in satisfaction. "It's not gone completely. But the knot is loosening. The spell's influence is fading. You'll see clarity soon Morgana. Soon."

Celeste clapped her hands together. "And if you start to panic just picture me yelling every possible insult at you in rhyme form. Works every time."

Morgana rolled her eyes but smiled genuinely. *I think I can survive that. I think I can survive this.*

As her friends left with Aurelia placing the remaining herbs carefully in Morgana's basket and Celeste giving one last dramatic bow Morgana felt the weight on her shoulders ease slightly. *I'm not alone. I have allies. I have guidance. I can face whatever comes next.*

But even as she washed the dishes one last time the image of Evander's lingering gaze pressed on her mind. *Will he still look at me like that when this is over? Will it be real or just the faint echo of magic fading?*

She closed her eyes and took a deep steadying breath. *I will find out. And when I do… I'll face it honestly. No spells and no tricks. Just the truth.*

The candle flickered gently casting soft shadows across the counter. Outside the streets of Eraldor were quieting for the night, but inside *The Golden Spoon* hope that was small, fragile, and trembling had begun to bloom.

Chapter 11 – A Magical Mishap

The bakery smelled of browned butter and yeast. It smelled like something thick and warm. It settled into every corner of *The Golden Spoon*. Morgana's hands hovered over the counter over the small bundle of herbs she had prepared with her nerves tightening with each passing second. Steam curled from the tea pot carrying the faint scent of chamomile and lavender, but it did little to calm her racing heart.

Focus. You can do this. Just a small counter-charm. Gentle. No fireworks.

She had spent last night practicing the visualization Aurelia had taught her. From the herbs, the tea, the candle, and the intent of unwinding the spell without forcing it. Now it was time to try it in the real bakery where her magic could meet reality.

Her heart thumped as she placed a small bundle of lavender, chamomile, and rosemary near her workstation. She lit a single violet candle letting the flicker illuminate her careful preparations.

"Deep breaths," she whispered to herself inhaling the faint calming aroma of the herbs. *Imagine the threads loosening. Imagine it unwinding. Gentle. Soft. Do not force it. Do not panic.*

Evander entered the bakery then just as he often did unaware of her plan. He leaned casually against the counter as his eyes followed her movements with a quiet curiosity that made her stomach tighten.

Do not fail. Please do not fail.

Morgana extended her hands with her palms down over the bundles of herbs. She murmured the incantation softly with the syllables wrapping around her intent like a warm ribbon. The air thickened with the scent of lavender and chamomile. Steam curled upward from the tea pot she had set to boil earlier.

For a moment everything seemed… perfect. The gentle pull of magic, the calm rhythm of her breathing, and the reassuring presence of Evander nearby. She allowed herself a small smile.

And then with a faint *pop* like a tiny burst of fireworks chaos erupted.

Flour leapt from the counter in soft white clouds and hovering midair as if caught in invisible hands. Sugar crystals glittered like tiny stars scattering across the floor and countertops. The herbs twirled in spirals, rising into the air before settling haphazardly back into their bundles.

Morgana froze with her hands still extended. *No. No, no, no. This was supposed to be gentle! Gentle! Not flour raining from the ceiling!*

Evander blinked once then laughed. It was a soft genuine laugh that made her ears burn hotter than any misfired spell could. "Morgana," he said with his voice warm but teasing, "you're turning the bakery into a winter wonderland. Are the customers going to help you clean or just watch in awe?"

Morgana's cheeks flamed. *Laughing at me? Of course he's laughing at me. My counter-charm backfired and now I'm a spectacle.*

"Evander!" she snapped though her tone trembled with panic. She waved her hands in a futile attempt to contain the flour. "I can fix it! I can—"

She tripped over her own feet, sending a tray of buns sliding across the counter. They bounced harmlessly into a basket, but the sound of them skidding across the wooden surface was enough to make her groan. *Wonderful. Just wonderful. Magic always finds a way to humiliate me.*

Evander stepped closer tilting his head as he observed the floating sugar and swirling herbs. "Do you need a hand? Or are we supposed to admire the spectacle?"

Morgana's eyes widened. *He's being calm and that makes it worse. If he were angry I could apologize and it would be over. But this amused him. He's enjoying this.*

"I... I don't—" she stammered trying to regain her composure. She muttered another half-hearted charm hoping to reel in the errant flour, but the attempt only made a few sugar crystals spin faster and then glitter across Evander's sleeves.

"Oh now you're decorating me," he said, laughing as he brushed the sparkling sugar off his arm. "Very considerate of you."

Morgana groaned and buried her face in her hands. *Why did I think I could control magic in public? Why did I ever think this was a good idea?*

Evander crouched slightly down as he picked up a handful of flour that had settled near his shoes. "It's... kind of beautiful in a messy and chaotic way," he said as he brushed some into his palm and let it drift through the air. "Almost like fireworks."

He's comparing my disaster to fireworks? I'm doomed.

"See? This is why I'm terrified of making mistakes. They don't just stay in the kitchen, but they spill everywhere." Morgana rushes out.

He gently chuckled. "It's not so bad."

Morgana's counter-charm should have worked. It *would* have worked on any other spell. But love magic didn't follow rules. It was temperamental, reactive, and almost alive. Every attempt to dampen it only made it lash out harder like trying to smother a grease fire with water. The more she pushed then the more violently it resisted.

This is why practitioners avoid it, she thought desperately as a cream puff launched itself across the room. *It doesn't want to be controlled.*

The little bell above the door jingled then and a few early customers peeked in. Their expressions ranged from curiosity to amusement as they noticed the suspended clouds of flour and the sparkling sugar drifting lazily through the air.

"Oh is this part of the demonstration?" one asked stepping inside.

"Yes!" Celeste's voice rang out from the corner where she had appeared seemingly out of nowhere, holding a tray of pastries she had "rescued" from the chaos. "Step right up folks! Watch Morgana attempt magic live! It's nothing but a fun little show."

Morgana spun toward her friend totally mortified. *Celeste! Now?! Why is she here?!*

Celeste gave a small shrug beaming. "I thought you could use a little… audience support."

Aurelia arrived behind her carrying a small bundle of unscathed herbs. She raised an eyebrow at the swirling flour and sugar then gave Morgana a small and reassuring smile. "Minor backfire," she murmured. "Nothing you cannot fix. Slow your breathing. Focus. It's still under your control."

Morgana swallowed hard and took a deep breath, trying to calm the surge of panic. *Focus. Gentle. Control. I can do this.*

She extended her hands again, whispering the soft counter-charm, and imagining the threads of magic unwinding instead of flaring. Slowly and tentatively the flour began to settle. The sugar sparkles drifted down like harmless confetti. Even the herbs returned to their bundles though a few leaves remained fluttering gently in the air.

Evander clapped softly still smiling. "Well done," he said. "I must admit, I'm impressed. You turned a simple morning in the bakery into a spectacle worthy of some kind of magic festival."

Morgana's face burned. *He's impressed? Or amused? Or both?*

"I—thank you," she muttered to him while still trying to shove floating flour back onto the counter with her hands. *Do not think about how he's smiling at you. Do not think about it. Do not—*

Evander leaned closer and brushed a stray spot of sugar off her cheek with his fingertip. Her heart lurched. *He's touching me again. And laughing. I... I can't think straight.*

Celeste clapped her hands. "Oh stop fretting! Look at it this way. If anyone deserves to look this embarrassed it's you. And also I'm recording it in my head for later stories. Epic fail or epic magic? Hard to say."

Morgana groaned audibly. *I am never living this down.*

Aurelia handed her a small cloth to clean the counter. "Mistakes happen. Even the most skilled magic users have minor disasters. The important part is how you recover."

She nodded before taking a slow breath and focusing again. *Recovery. That's all I can do. Calm. Gentle. Undo what I've done without making it worse.*

For the next several minutes she carefully guided the residual magic back into the herbs. She gently whispered soft, but deliberate words. Evander hovered nearby. He assisted by stepping aside when necessary and giving her occasional encouraging nods and amused smiles.

By the time the last floating sugar crystal fell to the counter Morgana's arms trembled, but she had succeeded. The bakery was restored to relative order except for a few tiny glittering specks of sugar that stuck stubbornly to the wooden counters and Evander's sleeves.

"You know," he said as he brushed some from his hand, "you make chaos look enchanting."

He's going to say it again. He's going to smile like that and I'm going to melt.

"I didn't mean for it to…" she began then trailed off. Words failed her entirely.

Celeste grinned leaning against the counter. "You didn't mean for it to be spectacular? Don't sell yourself short my dear. It's quite a show. And you looked adorable while panicking."

Morgana's blush deepened. She could feel heat creeping from her ears to her neck. *Adorable. I am not adorable. I am flustered, panicked, and embarrassed. Maybe all at once.*

Aurelia placed a comforting hand on her shoulder. "You are learning Morgana. Minor backfires are normal. What matters is your intent. You did this with care and awareness. That counts for everything."

Morgana exhaled shakily finally allowing herself a small tired smile. *Maybe I can manage this. Maybe magic isn't entirely a curse...*

Evander leaned closer, lowering his voice just enough that only she could hear. "Though I must admit seeing flour floating like that... I wouldn't mind it happening more often."

Heat roared through her again and she looked away focusing on sweeping the remaining sugar off the counter. *I am never going to live this down. And yet... I don't mind him laughing at me. Not entirely.*

The bell above the door jiggled as a few late customers peeked in catching the last hints of sugar glitter in the air. They smiled and murmured amongst themselves clearly charmed by the spectacle unaware of the delicate, but chaotic magic that had just unfolded.

They only thought it was a regular baking mishap not something magical in nature. There was no risk of them finding out the truth. *She was safe for now.*

Morgana straightened taking a deep breath and steadying her hands. She had survived her first real counter-charm in public. And though it had gone... spectacularly wrong she felt a tiny spark of pride flicker in her chest. *I am learning. I am growing. And perhaps I can control this magic without losing myself or him in the process.*

Evander's gaze lingered warm and amused as he finally stepped back to give her space. Morgana's cheeks burned, but a soft smile tugged at her lips. *Maybe it's worth the risk. Maybe magic even messy chaotic magic can be beautiful.*

Chapter 12 – Evander's Curiosity

The last of the evening's warmth still clung to the bakery stones with the ovens cooling slowly as shadows stretched long across the tiled floor. Morgana wiped her hands on her apron and exhaled relieved at the rare quiet. *The Golden Spoon* was closed, the last customers gone, and Agnes and Tomas had retired upstairs.

That left only her and Evander lingering as though neither wanted to break the spell of stillness.

He leaned against the counter. His dark hair kept falling into his eyes as he watched her with that half-smile that made her cheeks prickle with heat. "You work harder than anyone I've met," he said softly. "Do you ever stop?"

Morgana laughed under her breath tying the strings of her apron a little tighter just for something to do. "Someone has to keep this place from collapsing into flour and crumbs."

His gaze didn't move. It didn't even waver. "But what about you? Do you ever stop long enough to think about what you want?"

The question snagged at her like a loose thread. She looked down quickly to brush stray flour from the counter as though cleaning might erase the heat spreading in her chest.

What I want? Her mind filled too easily with forbidden images. She thought about a touch that lingered, a smile meant only for her, and the way his laugh seemed to chase shadows from the room. But those were dangerous wishes tangled with magic she had never meant to unleash.

She managed a half-hearted shrug. "I suppose... baking is what I want. It's what I've always wanted. Creating something with my hands that makes people smile. It feels like enough."

Evander tilted his head. "That's an answer you give customers. Not me."

Her breath caught. She forced herself to meet his eyes and nearly lost her nerve when she found him watching her with something softer than teasing. She scrambled for safer ground.

"You want recipes?" she asked quickly, reaching for a notebook she kept beneath the counter. Its leather cover was worn from years of powder-kissed by flour fingers.

His knowing smile spread. Now it looked amused. "I asked about your life, but recipes will do for now."

Morgana rolled her eyes but flipped the book open anyway smoothing the creased pages. "This one," she said as she tapped a page covered in neat handwriting and little doodles of sugar roses, "is my favorite. Honey-almond tarts. They were the first thing I baked that didn't collapse into a disaster."

Evander leaned in with his broad shoulder nearly brushing hers as he studied the inked notes. The proximity made her pulse skip. She could smell the faint scent of cedar on his coat and the warmth of him chasing away the bakery's chill.

"They look complicated," he murmured as he looked it over.

"They're not," she replied quickly glad to talk about something she could control. "It's all about patience. If you rush the honey it burns. If you fold the dough too quickly it toughens." She traced the steps with her finger lost in an old memory. "My mother used to say baking was like listening. The ingredients tell you what they need if you're patient enough to listen."

Her throat tightened on the last words. She hadn't spoken of her family in years and definitely not out loud. Evander's eyes softened as though he heard the unspoken weight behind them.

"Do you miss them?" he asked gently.

Morgana hesitated. The truth pressed hard against her ribs. *Yes every day. Yes in ways I can't explain. Yes, but I can't tell you how deeply magic was tied to our home.*

She swallowed. "Sometimes," she said carefully. "But the kitchen feels like home too. It's where I feel closest to them."

Evander's hand brushed against hers on the counter. It wasn't quite a touch, but enough to send her heart stuttering. His voice was low and sounded thoughtful. "That sounds less like baking and more like love."

Heat rushed into her face. She turned quickly, busying herself with closing the book. *Why does he have to say things like that? Why does it sound so simple when he says it as though love were something I could knead into dough and sugar?*

"Recipes are safer than people," she muttered and immediately regretted it as soon as the words left her lips.

But instead of laughing Evander's gaze deepened. "Maybe. But safer doesn't always mean better."

Silence stretched between them heavy with unspoken questions. Morgana's chest ached with the weight of what she couldn't confess. That his growing warmth toward her might be shaped by magic and not choice. That her heart was caught between longing and guilt. It was tangled in threads she couldn't untangle without risk of exposure.

He broke the silence with sudden levity. "All right then. If I wanted to impress someone which recipe would you give me?"

The abrupt change made her blink. "Impress someone?"

"Yes," he said smoothly though his eyes glimmered with mischief. "Say I wanted to cook for maybe a friend. Someone I hoped to make smile."

Her lips twitched. "You? In the kitchen?"

He placed a hand over his heart looking mock-wounded. "You doubt me?"

"I know you," she countered with laughter breaking through her nerves. "You'd burn water."

"Untrue," he said as he straightened dramatically. "I once made porridge. It was only mildly inedible."

Her laughter spilled out before she could stop it. It was light and unguarded. The sound echoed against the stone walls warming the bakery in a way no oven could.

When her mirth faded she realized he was still watching her. His smile looked softer now. Almost reverent. Her breath faltered.

Stop looking at me like that.

She turned abruptly, stacking pans on the shelf. "For impressing someone... shortbread is simple enough. Sweet without trying too hard."

Evander moved closer. His tone was teasing but threaded with something else. "And what would impress you?"

Her hands froze on the pans. *Don't answer. Don't let him see how much you wish he'd ask you in earnest.*

"I'm not the one being impressed," she said quickly as she halfhazardly pushed the pans into place.

He chuckled under his breath, but didn't press her further. The sound filled the quiet like the fading glow of embers and Morgana's chest tightened painfully.

As she blew out the lanterns one by one her thoughts swirled dangerously. *Why does he want to know about me? Why does it feel so good when he asks? And why do I ache to tell him everything even when I know it could ruin us both?*

She stole one last glance at him before the bakery slipped into darkness. His profile was outlined faintly by the early moonlight spilling through the windows steady and warm.

Her heart softened melting like sugar left too long near the fire. And for one fleeting and dangerous moment she wished the magic weren't to blame. And that this was simply Evander choosing to care for her all on his own.

Afterwards Morgana made her way to the market square that was nearby. She didn't have any errands or shopping needs. She just wanted to keep up public appearances and look to the community members as someone normal with nothing suspicious going on.

The square was packed with people and stall keepers. Every market gathering was like this. People gathered to gossip together more than actually shop. One could find anything that they wanted for sale here.

The market was thinning out for the evening with the lanterns flickering to life. Tomas Fairbain lingered by the fishmonger's stall. He lingered there not because he needed herring, but because he'd seen Morgana earlier slipping through the crowd with her basket clutched to her chest as though she carried gold instead of flour.

He narrowed his eyes and closely watched her. Morgana greeted a neighbor happily. Her laugh seemed bright and easy, but Tomas had lived long enough to know the difference between laughter and performance. She was nervous and people only smiled that wide when they were hiding something.

She ducked around the side street near the bakery's back door. Tomas adjusted his cap, muttered a farewell to the fishmonger, and followed at a distance.

From the shadows he saw her enter the bakery kitchen. She paused and glanced over her shoulder once as though to make certain no one was watching before slipping inside.

Tomas's jaw tightened. He didn't trust secrecy at all. He grew up being suspicious about peoples' behavior. While he was always friendly he was also naturally suspicious of people. It was born from his natural instinct for self preservation.

He moved closer listening through the door crack. The faint clatter of mixing bowls and...something else. A low hum like the faint ringing of glass after it's struck. Magic always carried a sound whether people admitted it or not.

His hand curled into a fist. "I knew it," he muttered under his breath.

Chapter 13 – Unexpected Help

The morning light slanted pale through the bakery windows carrying with it the scent of dew-damp cobblestones and the first stirrings of Eraldor's streets. Morgana moved listlessly from oven to counter. Her hands performed their tasks out of habit with her thoughts drifting somewhere far away. The dough had risen just right, the crusts were taking on their familiar golden sheen, and the pastries in the glass case looked near perfect. And yet nothing felt steady inside her.

The memory of the counter-charm gone wrong still burned in her chest, replaying again and again. She thought about the floating flour, the sparkling sugar, and the laugh that had tumbled so easily from Evander's lips while her face went scarlet. He hadn't mocked her not once, but the kindness in his laughter almost made it worse. It was the reminder that he saw her even when she wanted nothing more than to hide. *He sees too much. What happens when he sees the rest?*

She stacked a tray of shortbread with more force than necessary and she heard the metal clattering against wood. That was when a voice warm and steady drifted in from the doorway.

"You're carrying your thoughts in your shoulders again."

Morgana startled and turned. Tomas Fairbairn stood there leaning on the doorframe with one hand. His hair that was as white as sifted flour stuck up in odd tufts from the early morning and his apron already bore the familiar streaks of dough though the day had barely begun. His eyes which were sharp still despite the years were fixed on her with a knowing gentleness.

"Am I?" she asked him and attempted lightness though she couldn't disguise the weariness edging her voice.

He stepped inside with the limp in his gait steady but sure. "Aye. Same as Agnes when she's stewing on something she won't say. Her shoulders rise up like bread left too long to proof. Yours go stiff as a poker."

Despite herself Morgana let out a small laugh. "I'll have to practice better disguise."

"You'd be wasting time," Tomas said with a shrug. "Truth has a way of showing itself whether you like it or not."

The words pressed against her chest far too close to the secret she bore. *If only you knew how much I'm hiding.* She busied her hands by dusting crumbs from the counter, but Tomas only watched her as patient as ever.

"Come," he said after a moment. "The ovens won't mind if you sit a spell. I've a story to tell and you might do well to hear it."

Something in his tone sounded inviting and it drew her in. She hesitated and glanced toward the oven where the loaves were baking then finally nodded. She untied her flour-dusted apron and followed him to one of the small tables they had in the back of the kitchen for breaks.

The morning sun pooled gold over the table catching in the swirls of dust motes in the air. Tomas settled heavily into his chair, folding his calloused hands with the skin browned and lined from years of kneading dough. He looked out toward the street a long moment before speaking as though drawing his memories into focus.

"When I was your age," he began, "I had a choice to make. One I thought might break me."

Morgana tilted her head. Tomas's stories often came in small bursts. They were often jokes about Agnes and small anecdotes about customers, but this tone was different from the past. It carried weight.

"My family had a farm in the north," he went on. "Cold stubborn land. Soil black as soot, but hard as stone. The winters dragged long and the winds cut sharper than any knife. I was meant to inherit it. To work the fields like my father and his father before him. That was duty. That was blood."

As he spoke Morgana could almost see it. The endless gray skies, the ground resisting every seed pressed into it, and a boy with aching hands pushing on because he had no choice.

"My father was a man of the earth," Tomas said as his voice softened with memory. "Strong as an ox and proud as they come. He'd wake before dawn to break the frost from the fields, come home with mud up to his knees, and still call it an honest day's work. He believed a man's worth was in his sweat. And he wanted the same for me."

Tomas smiled faintly, but it was tinged with sadness. "But I... I dreamed different. Not of plows and fields, but of flour. Of the smell of bread rising in the oven. A strange thing eh? A boy dreaming of crust instead of crops. But every time my mother baked I'd sit by the hearth and watch. The scent of yeast and smoke and the golden crack of the crust lit something in me I couldn't put out."

Morgana felt her throat tighten. She knew that pull. That inescapable tug toward creation. *Just like magic calls to me.*

"One winter," Tomas continued, "I told my father. I said I didn't want the farm. I wanted to be a baker. You should have seen his face. His jaw clenched. His eyes... I thought he'd strike me down where I stood. He said I was turning my back on my blood and shaming the family. He said baking was woman's work not a man's. He near disowned me then and there."

Silence settled between them for a moment. It felt heavy as stone. Morgana's heart twisted at the thought. *Did he feel the same fear of rejection? The same weight of knowing his truth would hurt the ones he loved?*

"I left anyway," Tomas said quietly. "Packed a small sack and I went south. No coin and no certainty. Just a stubborn heart." His lips curved in a smile now, softer. "And that's when I met Agnes. She had flour on her cheeks and fire in her eyes. She said she'd never seen a lad so foolish as to think he could knead dough without tearing it to bits. She taught me. She was patient though I burned the first three loaves to ash. We made a right mess of things in those days. The flour was so thick in the air you'd choke with dough sticking to everything but the pan. But every ruined crust tasted like freedom to me. Like I'd chosen life with my own two hands."

His eyes softened further. Warmth radiated from him as though he were back in those early days. "And when my father saw years later what we'd built he softened too. He took in this little shop and the people lined at dawn for bread warm from our ovens. He never said he was proud, but... he came for tea once. And he smiled when he thought I wasn't looking. That was enough."

Morgana swallowed hard, blinking back a sting in her eyes. She had never heard him speak so openly of his past and the picture he painted clung to her chest. The frost-bound farm, the suffocating expectation, the leap into uncertainty, and the taste of freedom in burnt crusts was all her story just in another form.

The hiding, the longing, the terrifying honesty of choosing your own path even if it broke the ones you loved.

Tomas leaned forward now. His gaze was steady on hers. "The point lass is this: honesty costs. Aye it does. It near cost me my family. But hiding yourself? That costs more in the long run. You wake each day and live half a life until there's nothing left of you but shadows."

Her breath hitched and she looked down at her hands where flour had settled into the fine lines of her skin. *That's what I'm doing. Hiding. Living half a life. And one day there will be nothing left but the shell of what I wanted to be.*

Tomas didn't press her, but his eyes were kind and unyielding. "I see the way you care for this place. For us. For him." His glance flicked toward the lobby where Evander's humming carried faintly.

Heat flushed her face. "I—"

Tomas lifted a hand gently, stopping her. "You don't need to say it. Just remember this: if your heart is tangled don't cut it to pieces trying to make it neat. Better to face the knots, slow and patient, and work them out. Like dough that needs time to rise."

A laugh slipped from her lips. It sounded shaky but it was also real. "You always find a way to compare life to bread."

"It's the only language I speak," he said with a wink. Then his face softened again. They looked grave. "But Morgana lass don't let fear keep you silent. If you care for someone don't let them walk blind. People deserve to choose with truth not illusion."

The words struck like a bell ringing through her chest. *Truth not illusion.*

She thought of Evander's warm glances, his lingering touches, the way her heart leapt when he laughed. *Was it him? Or was it the spell she had loosed by mistake?* The question haunted her and yet Tomas's story lit a fragile thread of clarity inside her. Perhaps she couldn't keep hiding. Perhaps honesty even if it cost her would be kinder in the end.

Her voice came out in a whisper. "But what if honesty breaks everything?"

Tomas's gaze gentled with lines deepening around his eyes. "Then it wasn't built to last. But if it's strong enough then honesty won't break it. It will temper it. Like steel in the fire."

Her throat tightened painfully. She could feel gratitude and fear tangling within her. "Thank you," she whispered, the words barely holding.

He reached across the table with his rough warm hand covering hers. "Aye lass. You'll find your way. Just don't forget you've people who care for you here. You're not alone."

For a moment Morgana sat very still, letting the weight of his hand anchor her and letting the warmth of his words seep into her bones. Then the bakery's bell jingled suddenly announcing a customer. She rose quickly and brushed at her eyes before anyone could notice. Tomas eased himself up more slowly with his limp being steady but sure and with his smile carrying a quiet pride.

As Morgana returned to the counter her heart thudded unevenly. She felt Evander's gaze on her as she emerged from the kitchen. His smile was easy and unknowing and warmth rushed through her chest. But this time instead of flinching from the feeling she let herself hold it. It felt fragile and dangerous, but hers. For the first time she imagined a future where honesty might not destroy everything, but remake it into something stronger.

The bakery smelled of honey and warm crust. It was the kind of comfort that usually softened Tomas's edges. But tonight he lingered at the counter long after the last customer had gone. He patiently waited as Morgana wiped down the worktable.

"You've been busier than usual," he said casually though the words carried weight. His tone was too mild and careful.

Morgana didn't look up. "The festival's coming. People want sweets."

"Mm." Tomas studied her with the sharpness of a hawk. "Funny thing though. I could've sworn I heard you in here late last night. Humming maybe. Sounded like—" He tilted his head. "Well. Strange music."

Morgana's rag stilled on the wood for the briefest moment before she forced a smile. "You must've dreamed it. I went home early."

"Dreams don't usually smell of spice and sugar," Tomas muttered to her as he leaned on the counter. His eyes never left her face. "You're not overworking yourself are you? A tired hand makes mistakes. And some mistakes are harder to undo than others."

Morgana's lips pressed together. "I'm fine."

Tomas gave a slow nod as though he'd expected that answer. He straightened, lifting his cap from the peg near the door. "See that you are."

He left her there in the quiet bakery, but as the door clicked shut behind him Morgana felt the weight of his stare lingering.

Tomas's questions had been casual on the surface, but each one had prodded too close to the truth.

And he wasn't finished. She could feel it.

When the door finally shut and Tomas's boot steps faded Morgana sank onto the nearest stool. Her rag was still clutched in her hand. Her pulse thudded in her throat.

He knew. Or if he didn't know he was circling close enough to it.

She buried her face in her palms as she could smell the remnants of the scent of flour and butter clinging to her skin. *Fool.* She should have been more careful. Should never have let herself hum while weaving the threads of magic into the dough. Tomas's ears were too sharp and his memory too long.

The thought made her stomach twist. He had trusted her—trusted her word that she would keep her gift out of the kitchen, that she would honor the rule they both knew was sacred. She had promised.

And now every cookie, every loaf, every sweet that bore even a shimmer of magic carried the risk of shattering that trust.

Morgana pressed her hands flat against the cool wood of the worktable, fighting the urge to weep. It wasn't just fear of discovery that gripped her. It was the sharper colder fear of seeing disappointment in Tomas's eyes. Disappointment from him and Agnes would hurt worse than anger.

She whispered to the empty room as though the shadows might listen. "I'll be more careful. I swear it. I won't let him find out."

But the promise sounded thin even to her own ears.

Chapter 14 – Baker's Secrets

The ovens glowed faintly in the quiet of *The Golden Spoon* their heat humming low and steady as the night settled in. Their warmth usually comforted Morgana. It was the kind of warmth that spoke of home and safety, but tonight it pressed against her like an unwanted hand that was too heavy and too close. She leaned against the counter with her palms braced on the powder-dusted wood and felt her heart beating like a storm she couldn't still.

Evander's face haunted her more insistently than any dream. She kept thinking of the way his eyes lingered on her and searched her as though she mattered beyond measure. The casual brush of his hand against hers sending sparks through her blood. His laugh was deep and warm and broke her composure while it left her flustered. All of it lit her heart and all of it was tangled in her mistake.

Would he have smiled at me like that without the spell? Would he have leaned so close? Or is every touch, every glance, every word nothing but a thread of magic pulling him closer?

The thought hollowed her. She had sworn never to let her magic seep into her craft and never to weave enchantments where people trusted her hands to shape bread and sweetness alone. And yet by some twist of fate she had done exactly that. The charm had spilled from her amplifying and binding itself to things it should not touch. Now every time Evander laughed or lingered near guilt gnawed at her ribs.

That morning he had leaned on the counter with his sleeve brushing flour across his wrist and asked her what her favorite recipe was. He hadn't meant it idly. His gaze had been too steady and too curious for that. Morgana had faltered, mumbling something about honey cakes, and hated herself for it. He had smiled anyway with sunlight slipping through lace curtains and her heart had hammered against her chest until she thought it might give her away.

She pressed her forehead to her flour-coated hands as she could feel her breath shaking. *I should tell him. I should confess. I should say it before this goes further and before I dig us both into something we cannot untangle.*

But the thought of it made her chest seize. What would his face look like if she confessed? Would his gaze turn cold and shuttered with distrust? Would he leave the bakery and never return? Never lean against the counter or smile at her again?

A memory surfaced unbidden like sugar dissolving in water. She was small again and no taller than the kitchen table of her childhood home. Her mother's hands guided hers as they shaped dough. Her mother's voice sounded gentle. "Magic isn't a toy little one," she had said, flour streaking her cheek as she bent close. "It listens to your heart more than your words. If your heart trembles so will your spell. If your heart longs then your spell may reach for what you do not mean." Morgana had nodded with her tiny hands sticky with dough not fully understanding. But her mother's words had soaked into her all the same.

The ache of remembering hollowed her chest. Her mother's face would never bend close again. Her voice would never whisper warnings or comfort. Morgana carried them alone now with echoes rattling inside her where no one could hear.

Another memory rose then. This one was sharper and tinged with shame. She had been ten. She was excited and desperate to impress her father by charming a loaf of bread to rise faster. The spell had burst too strong filling the kitchen with a yeasty froth that spilled over the table and floor. She had sobbed, ashamed, sure she had ruined everything. Her mother had found her there sticky to the elbows and hiccuping back her tears. But instead of scolding her mother had crouched low brushed dough from her hair and smiled. "Mistakes teach us where our hearts lean," she had whispered, kissing Morgana's damp cheek. "And one day your heart will lean toward someone who makes you want to share everything. When that day comes child you must choose fear or honesty. The truth may hurt, but it is the only gift worth giving."

The words still lived in Morgana's bones, but they cut deeper now. They felt sharper for the silence her mother had left behind. *Would she still tell me the same if she saw me here wrapped in a lie and tangled in magic I cannot undo?*

Morgana lifted her head, staring at the rows of cooling bread across the room. She imagined Evander's hands beside hers learning how to fold cinnamon rolls and dusting flour across his dark hair and laughing as though the world were light. She imagined confessing to him as her voice shook and her eyes downcast. She imagined him pausing the smile fading and trust draining away like water through a sieve.

Her throat closed. *What if he looks at me like I am a stranger? What if he walks away? I have already lost my family. I cannot bear to lose him too.*

She began to pace as her shoes whispered across the floorboards. Each step stirred her thoughts into tighter knots. What would rejection feel like? Cold and sharp like stepping barefoot into frost. What would acceptance feel like? Sweet and unbearable like biting into honey after a lifetime of plain bread. Both outcomes terrified her equally.

Her mother's voice seemed to follow her steps, echoing from the corners of memory: *Choose carefully, little one. Fear or honesty. But know that hiding will starve you more surely than hunger.*

Tears prickled at the back of her eyes, but she blinked them away. "Not tonight," she whispered to the empty bakery. Her voice shook thin as spun sugar. "Not tonight. Tomorrow perhaps. Tomorrow I'll be braver."

But she knew it was a lie. Tomorrow she would feel the same. Tomorrow she would watch Evander's eyes linger, feel her heart ache, and silence herself again. She was caught between longing and terror and no spell could free her.

The ovens hummed low with their heat fading as the night deepened. Morgana blew out the lamps one by one as shadows spilled across the bakery's tiled floor. The darkness pressed soft against her shoulders and she carried her silence like a stone in her apron pocket. It was heavy and unshakable. Yet as she locked the door and stepped into the night air the echoes of her mother's voice followed her still reminding her that sooner or later she would have to choose.

Fear. Or honesty.

And though she buried the thought as deeply as she could Morgana's heart whispered what she dared not admit aloud. That what frightened her most was not rejection, but the hope that Evander might stay even after everything.

It was well past dusk when Tomas returned quiet as a thief to the bakery. He told himself it was only to prove his suspicions unfounded, but that was a lie he didn't bother defending.

The kitchen smelled faintly of sugar and spice though the ovens had long gone cold. He lit a small lamp and searched the work table. Nothing at first glance. He only saw flour dust and the remnants of dough. But then stooping to pick up his dropped matchbook he saw it.

There was a small round cookie half-hidden in shadow where it had rolled under the table.

Tomas reached for it intending to toss it aside, but the moment his fingertips brushed its surface the air in the room changed. A faint vibration thrummed through his skin. It echoed up his arm into his chest. It wasn't heat. It wasn't static. It was magic.

He snatched his hand back breathing hard. The cookie sat innocently on the floor golden and sugar-crusted, but it radiated wrongness like a bell that would not stop ringing.

His face hardened. He didn't need to taste it. He didn't need further proof. Morgana had lied. She'd promised, sworn even, never to cross that line. And now here was the evidence humming in his hand like a curse.

Tomas closed his fingers around it and straightened with his lamp casting deep shadows across his face.

"Damn you, Morgana," he whispered softly as the words were thick with disappointment. "You knew the rule. And you broke it."

The hum lingered in his palm. He had never felt more betrayed.

Chapter 15 – Spell's Pull

The day began as so many others had. Sunlight was streaming through the tall windows of *The Golden Spoon* and dusting the flour motes in golden light. Morgana's hands moved by habit kneading dough until it sighed under her palms and shaping rolls that would later swell into soft perfection. To anyone passing by she looked the same as she always had: steady, focused, her apron dusted with flour like snow. But her heart beat in a rhythm that no bread could match. It was quick and uneven because Evander Grimshaw stood only a few feet away.

He wasn't usually there so early. Normally he arrived midmorning a few hours after the first rush of customers and sometimes carrying a book tucked under his arm or sometimes simply leaning against the counter with an ease that made Morgana's insides tighten. But today he had appeared almost at dawn striding in with a determination that startled her. And he hadn't left.

He lingered now with his sleeves rolled to the elbow and his broad frame taking up more space than the room had any right to offer. At first he'd only watched her with that soft intensity that made her cheeks warm. But then the attentiveness sharpened taking on an edge she hadn't seen before.

When a pair of children darted too close to her worktable, reaching for sugar-dusted buns cooling on the rack, Evander's hand shot out before she could react. He caught one boy by the collar. His hands were not rough, but firm as he said, "Mind yourself. She's working." His voice was low and controlled, but the children fled wide-eyed all the same.

Morgana stared at him with her fingers frozen on the half-shaped loaf. "They're only children," she said. She gripped the dough tighter and her knuckles whitened as though the small loaf could anchor her against the weight of his words.

"They shouldn't be underfoot," he replied while his gaze slid back to her. "What if you tripped with a hot pan? What if they spoiled your work? You deserve respect here."

Her heart fluttered torn between gratitude and unease. She knew he meant well, but his intensity unsettled her. He wasn't wrong. She did deserve care and perhaps even protection. But never before had Evander stepped so forcefully into her space defending her as though the bakery were a battlefield. She didn't know how to feel about it.

As the morning wore on it only grew more pronounced. When an older man who was one of the regulars complimented her honey cakes Evander's jaw tightened. His hand brushed her arm as he leaned in close enough that she caught the faint scent of woodsmoke clinging to him. "You shouldn't have to endure men staring at you like that," he said too softly for anyone else to hear.

Morgana blinked up at him with her pulse racing. "He only liked the cake," she whispered back. Heat flushed her cheeks half from embarrassment and half from the slightly dizzying thrill of being so close to him. The words felt fragile on her tongue as if admitting them might shatter the tender hope blooming in her chest.

"Doesn't matter. They don't see you the way they should." His hand lingered on her sleeve before pulling back, but the warmth of it remained searing her skin through the fabric.

What's happening to him? This isn't Evander. This is me. This is the spell.

The truth made her stomach churn. The more she tried to unravel her mistake the tighter it seemed to weave itself. She had thought the magic subtle at first. From sprinkles spelling out playful encouragements, an extra warmth in his laughter, to an extra beat in his gaze. But now... now it was steering him. Pulling him. Shaping him into something he might never have chosen.

Yet her heart betrayed her all the same. Each lingering glance, each protective word, each brush of his hand she felt them too keenly. She longed for them even as guilt hollowed her chest. *What if some of it was real? What if the spell only nudged him closer to what he already felt?*

She tried to push the thought away, but it stalked her throughout the day. When she bent to lift a tray from the oven Evander was suddenly there steadying her elbow as though she were fragile. When she wiped sweat from her brow he pressed a clean cloth into her hand before she even thought to ask. When she carried baskets of bread to the front he hovered close. His presence felt both reassuring and suffocating.

By the time dusk settled over Eraldor Morgana's nerves were frayed thin. She slipped into the storeroom under the pretense of gathering more flour, but really she needed air, space, silence. She pressed her back against the sacks of grain with her breath shallow and her hands trembling.

This isn't fair to him. He doesn't even know he's being pulled. He doesn't even know his choices aren't entirely his own. And I... I'm letting it happen. I'm letting myself enjoy it.

The memory of her mother's words echoed faintly. It was a voice she hadn't heard in years: *One day your heart will lean toward someone who makes you want to share everything. When that day comes you must choose fear or honesty.*

Morgana closed her eyes. The sting of tears felt so sharp. "I don't know how to choose," she whispered to the empty room. "I don't know what's mine anymore or what's his."

When she returned to the bakery floor Evander was waiting. His gaze softened at the sight of her though the sharp edge of protectiveness still lingered beneath. He reached for her hand as though it were the most natural thing in the world with his calloused fingers wrapping around hers.

"You work too hard," he said quietly. "Let me walk you home tonight."

Her breath caught. No man had ever said such words to her not like this and not with such gentle conviction. Her heart screamed yes, but guilt pressed heavy against it.

"I can manage," she said with her voice sounding thin. Her mind spun caught between the longing that made her stomach flutter and the stubborn guilt that weighed her down. *Why does it feel so easy to want him close and yet so wrong?* she thought with each heartbeat echoing the tension between desire and caution.

But his grip tightened just slightly. "I insist. It's not safe for you to walk alone at night."

Her pulse pounded in her ears. The bakery around them blurred and the lamplight bent into soft halos. His hand was warm and anchoring. She wanted to lean into it and to believe in it. And yet every beat of her heart reminded her that this wasn't entirely him. The spell had its claws in his veins tugging.

When the last of the customers had gone and the doors were bolted he remained at her side. He did walk her home, shadowing her steps through the cobbled streets of Eraldor. His voice filled the silence with little nothings like comments on the cool night air, the glow of lanterns in the windows, the hush of the river beyond the square. She listened, but her thoughts churned beneath the surface.

At her door he hesitated as his thumb brushed her knuckles. His eyes searched hers. They were steady and unreadable. For a heartbeat she thought he might lean down. That he might close the space between them. Her breath stilled, her lips parting, her chest aching. She wanted him to do just that.

Instead he whispered, "Rest well Morgana. I'll see you in the morning." His hand lingered a fraction longer before he let go.

When the door closed behind her Morgana pressed her forehead against the wood with her breath shuddering out.

This isn't fair. I want him gods I want him. But is it me he wants or the spell?

She slipped into her tiny room and the air was heavy with the scent of flour clinging to her hair and clothes. The bed looked impossibly empty, but she did not lie down. She sat on the edge with her hands folded tightly in her lap and staring at the floor until her vision blurred.

The spell was pulling him closer and binding him tighter. It was shaping his choices in ways neither of them could see clearly. And she was letting it happen. Attraction tangled with guilt until she could scarcely tell one from the other. Her heart was split between longing and fear.

Her mother's voice returned softer than breath and echoing from memory: *The truth may hurt child, but it is the only gift worth giving.*

Morgana curled forward pressing her hands against her eyes. Tears slid hot and silent down her cheeks. She wanted to be brave. She wanted to confess. But fear coiled tight whispering that honesty might shatter the fragile sweetness blooming between them.

And so she sat there in the dim lamplight torn and trembling as outside the spell pulled its invisible threads tighter around both their hearts.

Morgana nearly dropped the tray of rolls when the bakery door opened. She tried to make a batch whenever she could for the homeless population in the city. She thought they should have something sweet and fresh to eat. The ovens were cooling, the lamps dimmed low, and she thought the day was done. Until she saw Tomas standing in the doorway with shadows pooling around him.

There was something in his face that froze her blood.

"Tomas?" she asked him. Her voice sounded slightly too brittle. "You startled me."

He didn't answer. He walked forward slowly and deliberately and simply held out his hand. Resting on his palm was a single sugar-crusted cookie.

Her heart lurched into her throat. She gripped the tray tighter to stop her trembling. "Where did you—"

"Under the worktable," he said flatly. "It rolled there quiet as a secret. Until I picked it up."

Her knees felt weak. *He knew. He must know.*

"I can explain," she blurted, panic rising like a tide. "It was only once—just to test—"

"Don't." His voice was sharp like a blade cutting her words to pieces. "Don't insult me with explanations."

Morgana flinched.

"You gave me your word," Tomas said steady but low like thunder before a storm. "You promised this place would be clean. That no spell would ever touch the bread, or the sugar, or the hands that made them. And yet here it is." He closed his fist slowly over the cookie. "Proof that your word means nothing."

Tears stung her eyes feeling hot and humiliating. "I didn't mean any harm," she whispered. "It was just to help. To bring a little light. A little sweetness. People need that right now."

His gaze was unyielding. "People need honesty more than sweetness. They need trust. Once that's broken Morgana it can't be baked whole again."

She wanted to speak and to defend herself, but shame knotted her tongue. And beneath the shame pulsed something else. She felt anger that was small but sharp at how he looked at her as though she were a reckless child.

Finally Tomas set the cookie on the counter. It glittered under the lamplight too bright and too guilty.

"This stays between us," he said with each word sounding deliberate. "The town must never know. If they suspect magic here they won't taste wonder in their bread they'll taste fear. And fear spreads faster than fire. Do you understand?"

Her voice shook. "Yes."

He turned and paused briefly at the door. His shoulders sagged and when he spoke again his words were softer but carried far more weight.

"I'm not angry Morgana. I'm disappointed. More than I can say."

The latch clicked. He was gone.

Morgana stared at the cookie. Her breath was shallow and her throat tight. Shame burned hot in her chest. She had let him down and broken what little trust they'd built. But even as guilt wrapped around her like chains a quiet dangerous thought stirred.

If they could taste the joy and the comfort magic brought wouldn't that be worth the risk?

She pressed her hand against the counter to steady herself. Fear of discovery and fear of disappointing Tomas gnawed at her. And yet beneath it all a spark refused to die.

Chapter 16 – Coffee and Confessions

The streets of Eraldor were hushed when Morgana pushed open the door to the little coffeehouse near the square with the bell above jingling softly. A cool draft followed her in carrying the faint scent of roasted beans and polished wood. It was later than she should have been awake, but the restlessness in her chest had driven her from the warmth of her small room above *The Golden Spoon.*

Evander was already there seated at a corner table near the window with his hands wrapped around a steaming cup. The lamplight fell across his face, highlighting the curve of his jaw and the gentle shadow under his eyes. He looked as if he had been waiting though his posture suggested patience rather than expectation.

Morgana's heart stumbled. *Why am I here?* she asked herself though a part of her already knew. She slid into the seat opposite him smoothing her pants as she sat down and tried desperately to ignore the way her palms ached from nervous tension.

"Thought you might need company," he said softly as his voice carried that familiar warmth that made her stomach knot.

She nodded grateful for the excuse to breathe and to be near him without the chaos of the bakery around them. "I… I couldn't sleep," she admitted quietly as her fingers traced the rim of her cup. "Too many things on my mind."

He leaned back slightly studying her. "You always carry too much Morgana."

He knows me too well. Her chest tightened. She wanted to look away and to hide the blush that crept up her neck, but she couldn't. She hadn't wanted to leave the bakery yet here she was drawn by the pull of something she couldn't name. It was something that the spell had only made more insistent.

The coffeehouse was quiet except for the soft clink of spoons and the distant hum of a kettle. Morgana lifted her cup inhaling the bitter aroma and trying to steady herself. *I can't let him know. I can't tell him it's me who's changed him and who's pulled him closer. He has to be himself or this is all wrong.*

Evander's voice broke the silence. It sounded low and careful. "You look tired."

"I am," she whispered. "It's… been a long day."

He nodded with his eyes softening. "I suppose we all have long days." Then after a pause he added, "I've been thinking… about things I haven't said in a long time. About regrets."

Her chest constricted. She wanted to ask what he meant, wanted to hear him, wanted to open herself entirely, but a wave of guilt and fear pressed her down. *If I speak he'll see the truth. He'll see how I've tangled his heart with magic. And then… everything will fall apart.*

But she couldn't look away. He was speaking softly, earnestly, and the vulnerability in his tone drew her closer like the tide dragging sand toward the sea.

"I've made mistakes," he continued. "Choices I wish I could take back. Opportunities I let slip because I was too afraid, too stubborn, too proud. Sometimes I wonder if I'll ever be… enough."

Morgana's throat tightened. She wanted to reach across the table to tell him that he was enough that he always had been. But the

114

truth was heavier. *He's enough... but not for the right reasons. Not yet.*

"I think everyone feels that way," she said softly. Her voice was almost lost in the hum of the coffeehouse. "Even people who seem perfect. Even people who look like they have everything under control."

He lifted his gaze and his eyes locked with hers. "Even me?"

"Yes," she whispered. Her heart lurched. She wanted to reach for him, to brush the hair from his brow, to tell him the truth. Instead she sipped her coffee letting the heat anchor her. *I can't. Not yet. It's too soon. I need to figure out what's mine to give and what belongs to the spell.*

Evander's hand shifted slightly on his cup hesitating as if he wanted to say more. Then he leaned back and exhaled a little breath slowly. "I suppose I've always worried... that I'll hurt the people I care about most. That my own mistakes will ripple farther than I can control."

Her chest ached at the honesty in his voice. Every word drew her closer and made the guilt in her heart twist sharper. She wanted to tell him, to confess, to make things right. But even as her pulse quickened with desire she recoiled. *I can't. Not until I understand the spell, not until I know how much of him is him and how much is... me.*

He paused again. His eyes were soft but probing and she felt the weight of his trust pressing on her shoulders. "I feel... safer when I'm near you," he said quietly. "Even when I don't understand why. Even when I don't know what to expect next. There's a calm with you Morgana. And yet—" His lips pressed together as his eyes darkened with thought. "And yet I can't tell if I'm seeing clearly if I'm myself."

His words hit like cold water. She set down her cup before her shaking hands could betray her. *He knows. He can feel it. He feels the wrongness of what I've done.*

She shook slightly as she brushed her fingers along the rim of her cup. "Evander…" she began to say with her voice trembling, "you have to know… I…"

Her words caught in her throat. *How could she explain without revealing the truth she had hidden for so long? How could she confess that her magic however unintended had pulled him closer, made him more protective, more attentive, more… himself in ways she had never allowed naturally?*

Evander's eyes softened further as if he sensed her hesitation without needing explanation. "Whatever it is," he said gently, "you can tell me. I'll listen. I always listen."

The warmth of his words made her ache. She wanted desperately to speak, to let him see the truth, to unburden her heart, and yet terror rooted her in place. *If I tell him now it could ruin everything. If I don't I'll feel this guilt every day until it poisons us both.*

Instead she lowered her gaze tracing patterns in the condensation of her cup. The spell's pull hummed in the back of her mind, reminding her of its presence and its quiet insistence. Every heartbeat and every flicker of connection between them was tinged with the magic she could not undo.

"I… I care for you," she whispered finally. Her words were trembling on the edge of confession. "I care more than I should."

Evander's hand hovered near hers hesitating and she felt the pull of his own heart. The genuine part that was untainted by her spell was reaching for hers despite the uncertainty. "I care for you too," he said softly. "Always have."

Her chest constricted as she felt hope and guilt warring in equal measure. *Even with the spell? Even knowing I've tangled your feelings?*

He tilted his head reading her expression as though he could see the storm inside her. "I don't know why I feel this Morgana. I only know that when I'm near you I feel whole in a way I didn't before."

The honesty in his voice tore at her. She wanted to reach for him, to let herself be pulled into warmth and connection, to forget the weight of her magic for a fleeting moment. But the guilt gnawed at her like fire against her ribs.

If he knew he might hate me. If he knew he might walk away. If he knew...

She pressed a hand to her chest feeling the rapid thump of her pulse. "Evander," she whispered with her voice raw with emotion, "I want to tell you everything. But I'm afraid."

He reached across the table as his fingers brushed hers lightly. "Fear doesn't mean you're wrong," he said gently. "Fear means it matters."

Her lips trembled and for a moment she let herself feel it all. From the pull of his presence, the warmth of his gaze, the ache of longing, and the sharp guilt of knowing how she had influenced him. She wanted to confess. She wanted to unburden herself. And she wanted to be honest and brave and let the truth bloom between them like the first loaf of bread pulled from the oven.

And yet she stayed silent letting the warmth of his hand anchor her and letting his words settle like a fragile promise in her chest. The tension between them was electric feeling charged with desire and fear, with love tangled in magic, and neither dared to speak the whole truth.

As the night deepened outside Morgana sipped her coffee, letting the bitter warmth fill her and grounding her in the moment even as her heart ached with longing. Evander's gaze never wavered. It was steady and patient as if he knew she was wrestling with something far larger than either of them.

She wanted to tell him everything. She wanted to confess. She wanted to free him and herself from the invisible threads binding their hearts together. But tonight she could only sit across from him, sipping coffee, feeling the pull of love and guilt, and wonder if honesty could wait until the spell's grip loosened.

And as the clock ticked toward midnight Morgana realized something she hadn't allowed herself to feel fully before: she was falling deep and irrevocably for a man who didn't yet know the whole truth and she thought with a mix of hope and terror for someone who might forgive her for it if she ever dared to speak.

Chapter 17 – First Emotional Clarity

The bakery was quieter than usual the next morning with soft sunlight filtering in through the tall windows and casting rectangles of warmth across the tiled floor. Morgana moved through the space with careful precision as her hands were dusted with flour as she kneaded dough and shaped pastries, but her mind was elsewhere turning over every glance, every touch, and every word from the night before. Evander's voice was soft and honest and it still hummed in her memory. She thought of the way he had reached across the table brushing his fingers against hers and how it made her chest swell and ache at once.

She paused resting her hands on the edge of the counter and closed her eyes. I've done something reckless. I've let the spell entangle him and nudge his heart. And yet… Her mind circled the thought feeling hesitant and fragile. *Was it entirely the spell?*

Memories of the past nights played behind her eyelids. They were small moments when his attention had lingered longer than usual, when his protective instincts had surfaced, when his laughter had warmed her like sunlight. At first she had believed them all to be the magic's doing. It was like an invisible hand pulling strings she had no right to touch. And yet now a faint realization began to take root.

What if the feelings were there all along?

She remembered the first time she had noticed him noticing her. Not the spell and not the enchantments, but the way his eyes had followed her, the way he had waited for her to speak, and the way he had smiled at her without prompting. Every time she replayed it the evidence grew harder to ignore. Evander had been drawn to her before magic touched him. The spell had only clarified, amplified, and nudged but it had not created the foundation of his feelings.

A small warmth settled in her chest at the thought. It felt hesitant and fragile yet insistent. *Maybe there is hope. Maybe what I feel isn't all borrowed and isn't all mine imposed on him.*

She sank into a chair behind the counter where she pulled a small notebook from the drawer and then opened it to a blank page. She scribbled quickly almost desperately tracing the moments that had made her heart flutter: the way he had insisted she take a break when she worked too hard, the gentle concern when children crowded near her baking, the way his eyes softened whenever she spoke about recipes she loved. And slowly as her pen moved across the page she began to see the patterns, the threads that had existed before the spell, and the traces of him that were undeniably himself.

He notices me. Not because I enchanted him, but because he wants to.

Her hands shook slightly with the realization feeling both thrilling and terrifying. If the feelings existed independently then perhaps she could allow herself to hope. Not reckless and not naive, but careful, measured hope. And yet guilt still gnawed at her. *I've influenced him yes. I've let the magic touch him. But even with that he is still Evander still seeing me and still choosing me in some small undeniable way.*

Morgana closed the notebook, pressing her palms to her face. She remembered her mother again the voice so clear it was almost audible in the quiet of the bakery: *Your heart will lean toward someone who makes you want to share everything. You must choose fear or honesty.*

I can lean toward hope, Morgana thought. *I can let myself trust the parts of him that are real, even if the spell has complicated the rest.*

She exhaled slowly and the tension in her shoulders eased fractionally. Perhaps she didn't need to untangle every strand immediately. Perhaps the first step was to acknowledge what had always been there beneath the shimmer of magic. The genuine connection that had drawn them together long before she had miscast a charm.

The morning passed in a soft blur customers arriving with small orders, asking about the day's specials, and exchanging pleasantries with the elderly owners. Morgana moved through it all with her hands busy and her heart still lingering in the quiet moments of clarity she had carved out for herself. Evander appeared mid-morning his presence familiar and the spell's influence humming faintly but no longer suffocating. She felt relief at the steadiness of it. Feeling a gentle hope threading through her chest.

He approached the counter with a tray of tea he had insisted on bringing and then set it down carefully before her. "For you," he said softly as his eyes caught hers in that unflinching way she had come to both fear and crave.

"Thank you," she whispered as she felt her cheeks warming. She poured a cup, her hands steady for the first time in days, and gestured toward the small stool beside the counter. "Sit."

He did and for a moment they simply watched each other and let the silence settle like a soft blanket. There was no rush and no pressure. There was only the quiet acknowledgment of presence and the shared rhythm of breath and warmth.

Morgana sipped her tea feeling the heat seep through her fingers. "Evander," she began carefully, "I... I've been thinking. About us. About... everything that's happened."

His brow lifted as she saw curiosity sparking in his dark eyes. "Everything?" he asked gently.

"Yes," she said slowly while meeting his gaze. "I realized something. The spell that I accidentally did... it amplifies yes. It nudges emotions and makes feelings more intense. But it doesn't create them. Not entirely."

He nodded slowly. His lips curved together into a small smile. "I had suspected that," he admitted. "I felt... drawn to you yes, but it was never something I didn't recognize in myself. Even before..." He gestured vaguely to the both of them acknowledging without naming the magic. "Even before there were pieces of this... of me wanting to be near you."

Her chest tightened with hopeful relief. "So... you're saying some of this is real. Even with the magic?"

"Yes," he said simply. "I care for you Morgana. That's me. The rest... maybe it's more complicated, but it doesn't change the core."

Tears pricked her eyes, but they were tears of release rather than guilt. The knot in her chest loosened fractionally allowing a sliver of hope to shine through. *He sees me. Even with everything tangled he chooses to see me.*

They sat together talking in low tones sharing fragments of life, memories, and small confessions. Morgana found herself laughing softly at something he said about an early baking disaster feeling the warmth of connection without the shadow of manipulation pressing down. Every word and every shared glance reinforced the truth she had feared to admit: Evander's heart had its own will, its own affection, and was entirely independent of the spell's shimmer.

She reflected on the past weeks and on the chaos the magic had wrought from the tension, the mistakes, the blushes and awkward stares, and the spells gone awry. And yet now clarity emerged through the fog. The emotions had been there all along quiet and steadfast just waiting for recognition. The spell had merely pulled the thread taut revealing the pattern that had existed from the beginning.

I don't have to feel guilty for what is real, she thought. *I don't have to hide from him, or from myself. Not entirely.*

Her gaze softened as she looked at him, taking in the familiar line of his jaw, the warmth in his dark eyes, and the gentle curve of his mouth as he spoke. Hope mingled with longing. It was a delicate blend that made her heart ache with both desire and wonder. She had glimpsed something true amidst the chaos. Something that belonged to them both untouched by misfired magic.

The rest of the day passed in a slow comforting rhythm. Morgana worked, Evander assisted in small practical ways, and neither pushed too far. Neither demanded more from the other than the moment could bear. She felt a budding trust forming. It was tentative but real like the first signs of spring beneath melting snow. She allowed herself to savor it careful not to overreach and careful not to confuse hope with certainty.

As night approached Morgana closed the bakery, extinguishing the lamps one by one. She lingered a moment with her hands pressed to the counter thinking of the day's revelations, thinking of Evander, thinking of the first true clarity she had felt in weeks.

The pull of the spell was still present it was like a faint hum in the background, but it no longer dominated her every thought. For the first time she felt the beginnings of control not over him and not over the magic, but over her own heart.

This is real, she whispered to herself. *Some of this is real. And maybe that is enough for now.*

And with that thought Morgana felt a small but unwavering spark of hope ignite within her. It was a spark that might in time grow into something stronger something unshakable and something worthy of both truth and love.

Chapter 18 – Customer Curiosity

The morning crowd came early to *The Golden Spoon* as it always did. Farmers, merchants, and weary night-watchmen all seemed to funnel toward the smell of fresh bread and the promise of pastries dusted in sugar. Morgana moved behind the counter with practiced ease arranging loaves on the display rack and brushing a sheen of glaze over golden buns. The air was rich with cinnamon, yeast, and melted butter. It was a symphony of scents that never failed to draw smiles.

But today as she worked she could feel the difference. It wasn't in the bread or the bustle of voices, but it was in Evander.

He stood near her side closer than necessary. His large hands steadied a tray she could have carried herself. He brushed flour from her sleeve when she spilled it and leaned close to murmur reminders when she forgot to wipe her hands before greeting a customer. To anyone else it might have seemed natural and helpful even. But Morgana knew. She could sense the devotion in his smallest movements and the quiet intensity of his attention.

And apparently so could everyone else.

"Looks like our Evander's found himself a new calling," one of the farmers chuckled as he collected his loaf. His tone was good-natured and gently teasing, but Morgana felt the heat rush to her cheeks all the same.

Another customer, a middle-aged woman with a basket hooked over her arm leaned conspiratorially toward her as she accepted her change. "You know, dear I've never seen him so steady. Always thought he was too restless for bakery walls, but with you here..." Her eyes twinkled and her smile was kind. "Well perhaps I was mistaken."

Morgana ducked her head murmuring thanks and hoping the warmth in her face wasn't too obvious. Behind her Evander only smiled unfazed by the commentary as though he didn't notice or didn't mind.

By mid-morning the whispers had taken on a life of their own. Patrons lingered longer than necessary with their gazes flicking between Morgana and Evander as though the loaves and buns were only an excuse. Laughter was softer but knowing and conversations lilting with a subtle curiosity. *The Golden Spoon* had always been a place for gossip, but now Morgana found herself at the center of it.

It wasn't cruel. No one sneered or spoke with malice. If anything the tone was warm and approving as though they were delighted by what they saw. But for Morgana the attention pressed like too many eyes, heavy and uncomfortable.

She nearly dropped a tray when two younger women leaned together by the counter whispering not-so-quietly to each other.

"Look at the way he watches her."

"It's like she's the only thing in the room!"

"Do you think they're…?"

Morgana forced a polite smile as she handed over their purchase, her hands trembling faintly. *If only they knew,* she thought as her stomach twisted. *If only they knew it isn't as simple as that. It isn't as innocent.*

When the girls had left giggling to themselves Morgana pressed her hand to her apron as though she could calm her heart by sheer will. Evander appeared at her side a moment later steady as always carrying another basket of rolls. His presence should have soothed her like it often did, but today it only sharpened her unease.

"Are you all right?" he asked softly as his eyes searched her face.

"Yes," she lied quickly. Too quickly. She busied herself with rearranging the rolls her back stiff. "It's just… busy today."

He didn't press, but his hand brushed her arm. It was a fleeting touch that lingered in her skin long after he turned away.

By the time the lunch crowd trickled out and the bakery quieted Morgana felt wrung out. She wiped her hands on her apron and leaned against the counter letting the silence settle. Agnes and Tomas had retreated upstairs for their midday rest leaving her alone with Evander.

He leaned against the wall with his arms folded together loosely and watching her with that same quiet focus that had set half the city whispering by now. It wasn't hostile. It wasn't even demanding. But it was steady, unyielding, and everyone else had noticed.

Morgana groaned softly, covering her face with her flour-dusted hands. "They're all talking about us."

Evander's voice was calm and almost amused. "So?"

She peeked at him through her fingers feeling absolutely mortified. "So? You don't care that they're gossiping?"

His brow lifted slightly. "They're not gossiping cruelly. They're noticing. Is that so terrible?"

"Yes!" she blurted then immediately wished she could take it back. Her voice echoed too loudly in the empty bakery. She lowered it to a whisper. "It's embarrassing. They'll think… they'll assume…"

He pushed off the wall and stepped closer not menacing but undeniably certain. "They'll rightly assume I care for you." His tone was matter-of-fact. It wasn't a confession so much as a truth he had long accepted. "And they wouldn't be wrong."

Her breath caught. She turned away, pretending to busy herself with stacking plates though her hands shook. *Not wrong. But not right either. Not completely. If only they knew what binds us. If only they knew the magic tugging at his heart.*

But she couldn't say that. Not when the warmth in his voice sounded so genuine and so unburdened by doubt.

Instead she muttered, "It isn't professional."

His soft laugh brushed against her ear. "This isn't the royal court Morgana. It's a bakery. A place for warmth, for bread, for connection. People see what they want to see. And right now they see you and me standing together."

Her cheeks burned. She turned back to him at last meeting his steady gaze. His eyes were kind. Definitely not mocking and not dismissive. They looked kind and if she dared admit it sincere.

The knot in her stomach loosened just a fraction. Perhaps it wasn't ruinous. Perhaps the rumors were not daggers but threads weaving something she hadn't dared to name.

Still when she locked the bakery that night she lingered at the door staring out at the quiet street. The whispers of the day followed her with laughter echoing faintly in her ears. *They all believe he's devoted to me. They all think this is real. But how much of it is? And how much is the spell twisting the truth?*

Embarrassment warred with secret longing and guilt with fragile hope. She hugged her arms around herself, staring at the stars flickering into being above Eraldor's rooftops.

The city was alive with rumor now and she could not control it. Perhaps she didn't need to. But the thought that she was walking on a knife's edge, caught between truth and enchantment, would not leave her.

And as she made her way home through the lamplit streets Morgana realized something else. The city's whispers had only just begun.

Chapter 19 – The Second Ingredient

The kitchen was quiet save for the low hiss of the oven and the ticking of the wall clock. For once Morgana was grateful for the hush. Agnes and Tomas had gone upstairs to rest, Evander had promised to stop by later in the evening, and for now, *The Golden Spoon* belonged entirely to her. She leaned against the wooden counter staring at the array of bowls, jars, and neatly lined spices before her as though they might reveal an answer she hadn't yet found.

Her hands trembled as she reached for the flour jar. This was foolish reckless even, but necessary. The spell she had tangled Evander in had grown thicker like a silken rope tightening around them both. The look in his eye that unwavering devotion that seemed so absolute left her aching with doubt. *Was it real? Or had she stolen his heart with a careless pinch of enchanted sugar?*

She dusted flour onto the work surface and pressed her palms flat into it leaving faint handprints behind. "If the first charm brought too much... perhaps the second will balance it," she whispered. Her mother's voice faint and distant stirred in her mind. *Magic is neither good nor bad Morgana. It is intent that shapes it. Your intent must be clear and your purpose honest.*

Her intent tonight was balance. Neutrality. If the spell was amplifying Evander's emotions perhaps it could be softened and tempered until what remained was purely his.

She set to work with a baker's precision because that at least she could control. Butter was measured and softened, eggs cracked into a ceramic bowl, sugar whisked until it gleamed pale and frothy. But alongside the ordinary ingredients she laid out the uncommon ones: a sprig of dried valerian root for calming, a scrap of parchment inked with a sigil of unraveling, and a crystal vial filled with water she had gathered at dawn from the river outside Eraldor's walls.

Her fingers hesitated over the vial. The water shimmered faintly in the candlelight touched by the hush of morning and the absence of witnesses. If anything could wash clean what she had stirred into being it was this. She uncorked it and the faintest breath of cool air spilling from within and tipped a single drop into the batter. It rippled outward in concentric circles like a stone tossed into a pond.

Morgana swallowed hard and stirred. The batter thickened under the wooden spoon. It was fragrant with vanilla and cinnamon though there was something sharper beneath. There was a bright, almost metallic tang that wasn't entirely of this world.

Her heart raced. *What if this doesn't work? What if it makes things worse?* The thought pricked at her like nettles and she nearly set the spoon down. But then she pictured Evander's smile unguarded and warm. She pictured the way his hand brushed hers when he passed her the sugar tin and how his laugh rumbled in his chest. She wanted to know if that smile and that laugh belonged to him alone and not the spell's design.

So she pressed on.

The oven roared to life swallowing the muffins in a golden heat. Morgana leaned against the counter and pressed her knuckles into her lips, watching through the little glass window as the tops rose and split releasing tendrils of cinnamon-sweet steam. It should have been comforting. Instead she felt like she was standing at the edge of a cliff waiting to see if the wind would carry her upward or dash her against the rocks.

When the timer chimed she nearly jumped. The muffins were domed and perfect and their tops kissed with a beautiful bronze. She pulled them free with a cloth and set them on the rack to cool as the scent flooding the kitchen with warmth. They looked ordinary and totally innocuous. No one would suspect the threads of spell work woven through their crumb.

Morgana broke one open with gentle steam curling from its soft heart. She held it between her fingers, trembling. *Should I taste it first?* Her tongue felt dry and her stomach tight. *What if the charm backfired unraveling her own emotions instead? What if she emptied herself out until there was nothing left but a hollow shell of a baker?*

"No," she whispered shaking her head. "This isn't for me."

It was for him. For the truth.

The bell above the front door jangled faintly startling her. Morgana's heart leapt though she already knew who it would be. Evander stepped into the bakery. Hs dark hair was slightly tousled from the evening breeze and his smile seemed as steady and grounding as the hearth flame.

"You're still here," he said warmly. "I was hoping you would be."

Morgana brushed flour from her apron and tried to will her pulse to steady. "I was… experimenting."

He raised a brow and then stepped closer. "Experimenting? Should I be worried?"

"Only if you don't like muffins," she replied, forcing a lightness she didn't feel.

He leaned against the counter with his eyes glinting. "Then I have nothing to fear."

Her fingers itched as she set the plate between them with the muffins still warm. She watched as he reached for one unguarded and entirely trusting and the enormity of what she had done pressed against her chest. *You're giving him a choice*, she told herself. *You're giving him back his own heart if he wants it.*

Evander bit into the muffin with an appreciative hum. "Morgana this is…" He paused chewing slowly and his brow furrowing. His gaze flickered softer and puzzled. "…different. Comforting somehow."

Her breath caught. She searched his face for signs. She was looking for a slackening of that intense devotion or a loosening of the tether between them. But instead of fading his eyes only grew gentler.

"Do you like it?" she asked him. Her voice sounded hushed.

He smiled though more subdued than before. "I do. It feels… honest."

Something inside her cracked fragile and aching. Perhaps it was working. Perhaps the spell's grip was loosening just enough to reveal the truth beneath. And if the truth was still warm eyes and quiet smiles then maybe, just maybe she hadn't stolen everything after all. She desperately needed to know if he still chose to sit across from her with crumbs dusting his fingers after everything.

As the night stretched on they ate in companionable silence and Morgana's thoughts whirled like sugar dissolving in tea. She didn't know what tomorrow would bring, whether the neutralizing charm would hold, or if it would unravel into something unforeseen. But for the first time in weeks she felt a flicker of something steadier than guilt.

Hope.

Chapter 20 – Spells in the Shadows

Morgana Valehart had learned long ago that magic had a way of clinging. It seeped into cracks, clutched at seams, and lingered even when you swore you had scrubbed every trace away. She had spent the last week convincing herself her neutralizing charm, the one she had coaxed into a tray of muffins, had worked. Evander's smiles had softened and his touches were less charged. His words carried warmth that felt genuinely his instead of tangled up in something she'd forced.

And yet as dawn filtered pale gold through the bakery windows her chest was tight with unease.

She whisked cream for the morning's icing each turn of her wrist was steady and controlled. The silver basin sat ready beside her. It was a deep bowl polished by years of use. She tried to lose herself in the motion.

It worked. It had to have worked. I didn't ruin him. I didn't ruin us.

The whisk gave a twitch.

Morgana frowned and gripped it tighter. But before she could adjust the handle jerked against her palm. She gasped as the whisk wrenched itself free twirling in the bowl as though it had suddenly remembered a dance it had been waiting years to perform. Cream splattered her sleeve.

"Oh no. Oh absolutely not." She lunged, but the whisk darted just out of reach spinning with gleeful independence.

The cream bubbled unnaturally. Thick froth rose above the rim like a swelling tide. A white blob slopped over, crawling across the counter as if eager for escape. Morgana slapped it with her hand flattening it back into stillness.

This is fine. Just a small flare. Just—

The whisk zinged out of the bowl circling her head like a wasp.

"Stop that!" she hissed waving her arms. Her braid whipped across her shoulder with cream clinging in messy streaks to it.

From the front of the bakery Tomas hummed as he stocked the shelves with fresh loaves. Morgana's stomach dropped. If he saw so much as a floating crumb she'd be done for.

The whisk dove for her hair. She ducked as heart hammered.

And then the bell above the front door jingled.

"Morgana?" Evander's voice. Warm. Curious. Too close.

Her eyes went wide. "Not now. Definitely not now," she hissed at the whisk as if it were a naughty child. The utensil wobbled as though mocking her.

Why is it always him? Why does chaos always wait for the exact moment he walks in?

Evander's boots tapped softly across the floorboards closer to the magical chaos that was happening. She forced her voice into something resembling casual. "Just a moment!"

But the whisk was not interested in patience. It zipped past her ear, dove into the cream bowl again, and began whipping with manic energy. The mixture puffed up like a rising storm cloud glittering faintly.

"No, no, no— " Morgana grabbed a tea towel and flung it over the bowl. The whisk kept moving beneath thumping wildly like a trapped bird. Icing spurted out from under the cloth in sugary streaks.

"Morgana?" Evander stepped into the kitchen doorway. His brows lifted as he took in the sight.

She spun with her arms stretched wide to block his view of the work table. "Evander! You're early." Her voice pitched too high, cracking like a dropped plate.

He tilted his head as his gaze flicked past her shoulder. "What's—"

The tea towel launched into the air then. A fountain of cream followed it raining sugar-sweet droplets across the kitchen. One glob landed square on Evander's cheek.

Morgana froze.

He blinked at her in shock with cream sliding slowly down toward his jaw. Then he laughed. It was a rich warm sound that curled around her like firelight.

Her face flamed. *Oh gods, he's laughing, and I look like a lunatic wrestling frosting.*

"I didn't realize you had such enthusiastic ingredients," he teased while swiping the cream with his thumb.

Morgana's throat went dry. Her eyes dropped to the thumb and to the way he licked it clean without breaking eye contact.

Her heart thumped against her ribs. *No spell could do that. That's just him.*

The whisk gave another defiant spin before showering both of them with a final mist of cream before clattering to the floor spent.

Evander chuckled again, stooping to retrieve it. "Seems even your tools can't resist working harder for you."

Her cheeks burned hotter. "It happens."

"Does it?" His eyes glinted amused and curious. They were too sharp for her comfort.

Lies never tasted so bitter.

Before she could think of an excuse another problem announced itself.

A tray of unfinished pastries that were plain little rolls meant to be filled later quivered on the counter. One gave a determined wiggle then rolled off the tray entirely. It plopped to the floor with a muted thud. Then another followed. And another.

Evander turned his head to look at them totally bewildered. "Are they... escaping?"

Morgana darted forward and scooped up the wayward rolls as though they were naughty kittens. "Gravity. Slanted tray. Happens all the time." She forced a grin that felt like a mask about to crack.

But the pastries weren't finished. One bounced against her hand wriggling like it had bones of jelly. Another rolled in circles leaving a faint trail of sugar dust. The last leapt onto Evander's boot, clinging stubbornly.

He bent down plucking it off with a low laugh. "I think it likes me."

Kill me now.

Morgana wrestled the rest back into the tray pressing her palm firmly over them as if sheer weight could hide the twitch of magic beneath. "They just—sometimes the dough holds too much air."

Evander raised a brow still holding the clingy pastry. "This one's feisty. Should I... eat it into submission?"

She almost choked. "No! It's not baked properly yet."

Oh stars above this is going to spiral until I'm buried in butter and shame.

As if summoned by the thought the frosted sugar bowl rattled on the shelf. Tiny granules lifted like glitter caught in sunlight drifting lazily through the air. Sparkles floated between them suspended like stars.

Evander's gaze tracked the glimmer with his expression softening in wonder. "It's... beautiful."

Her stomach clenched. *It's dangerous.*

She slapped her hand over the bowl forcing the sugar to settle. "Draft," she croaked. "You know how old this place is."

He smiled at her with his eyes bright. "Drafts don't usually look like starlight."

Her pulse skittered. She forced herself to laugh brittle and sharp. "Then I suppose the bakery has a bit of magic in it."

The words slipped out before she could stop them. Her breath caught in her throat.

Evander didn't seem to notice the weight of them. He only leaned back pastry still in hand with his lips curved. "I think it suits you."

Her chest tightened. *Don't say things like that. Don't make this harder.*

The kitchen had settled mercifully. The whisk lay inert on the floor, the pastries stilled under her palm, and the sugar bowl quiet. But Morgana knew it was only a pause. It was like a held breath before the next ripple.

She wiped her cream-splattered cheek with the back of her hand. "I should clean this up."

"I'll help," Evander said immediately.

"No!" It came out too sharp. She softened it quickly. "I mean you're a customer. You shouldn't."

"I'm not just a customer." His voice was gentle and steady.

Her throat tightened. *No. You're not. And that's the problem.*

Evander reached out and brushed a streak of cream from her temple. His touch lingered soft and certain. Her heart gave a painful, but wonderful twist.

The bell jangled again at the front door. Tomas's voice carried back greeting another early riser. Morgana jerked back from Evander panic prickling her skin.

If Tomas or Agnes ever saw the truth from the sparks to the flying icing then everything would crumble.

She forced a smile. "You should go sit. I'll bring you something fresh."

For a long moment he studied her as the playful warmth in his eyes was edged with curiosity. Then he nodded and slipped back toward the front with the pastry still in hand.

When he was gone Morgana sagged against the table with her chest heaving. The sugar bowl rattled faintly mocking her.

This is getting worse. If I don't get control soon... the whole bakery will know.

Her gaze drifted toward the doorway where Evander had stood. Laughter was still echoing in her ears. Heat pooled low in her stomach tangled with guilt.

And if he finds out before I tell him myself... will he ever forgive me?

Chapter 21 – Evander's Vulnerability

The bakery had quieted for the evening. Its usual hum was reduced to the faint tick of cooling ovens and the slow drip of coffee from the pot Morgana had insisted on making "just for the two of them." The world outside had dimmed to twilight blues and softened lamp glow, but inside *The Golden Spoon* the air was steeped in warmth and the faint sweetness of caramelized sugar that still clung to the rafters.

Evander sat across from her at one of the small corner tables. His posture was relaxed in a way she rarely saw during the rush of daylight hours. A mug rested in his hands, steam curling in lazy ribbons between them. His eyes that were usually dark, steady, and always carrying some private storm looked almost younger in this soft light.

Morgana watched him over the rim of her own mug as every one of her nerves thrummed with unease. *This is dangerous. I can't let him get too close. Not like this. Not when I know the truth and he doesn't.*

But when he smiled faintly at her as though drawing courage from her presence, her heart betrayed her. She leaned in just slightly unable to help herself.

"I've never told anyone this," Evander began. His voice sounded low and thoughtful as though each word cost him effort. "Not even... well anyone."

Morgana's fingers tightened around her mug. "You don't have to," she said quickly. "If it's hard—"

"It is hard," he admitted as his eyes dropped to the coffee mug. "But you asked me once what I wanted out of life. What I dreamed of."

She swallowed nodding slowly.

His gaze lifted again and for a moment she saw something raw there. She saw a boy instead of the man who moved through the world with practiced ease. "When I was a child I lived on the outskirts of Greymoor. My family didn't have much. My father was a mason. He was always gone. Always building walls and houses for other people while ours sagged around us. My mother... she did her best. She worked herself sick just to keep food on the table."

He paused, shaking his head with a rueful chuckle. "I was small. Too small for my age. Easy to overlook. Easier still to push around."

Morgana's chest ached. She had always seen him as steady, grounded, and almost untouchable. But here he was pulling back the armor to show the bruises beneath.

"Children can be cruel," he said softly. "They used to take my lunch. Sometimes it was nothing but a crust of bread, but it was mine and they'd steal it. Push me down in the dirt. I tried to fight back once, but..." He laughed again sounding hollow this time. "I wasn't strong enough. Not then."

Morgana's hand twitched aching to reach across the table. *He's not the only one who knows what it is to be small. To be powerless. To be overlooked.*

"I used to hide," Evander continued. "In the alley behind old baker Fenton's shop. He was the only one who didn't run me off. Sometimes he'd toss me the heels of bread no one wanted.

Sometimes if he was in a good mood he'd let me sweep for scraps. That smell of bread hot from the oven…" His eyes softened as a wistful smile tugging at his lips. "It felt like safety."

Morgana blinked rapidly, her throat tightening. *Bread as safety. Sweetness as sanctuary. He knows. He understands more than he realizes.*

"I swore to myself that one day I'd build a life where no one could take that away. Where no one could push me into the dirt and laugh. I wanted…" He trailed off. His brow furrowed together as if ashamed of the admission.

"You wanted what?" Morgana prompted gently though part of her dreaded the answer.

"I wanted to belong," he whispered. "To someone. To something. To have a place at a table where no one questioned if I deserved it."

The words cut through her like a blade because they echoed her own secret longings too closely. The bakery had become her sanctuary yes, but she had never truly belonged here. Not with the Valehart name burned into her past and not with the secrets heavy in her hands every time she kneaded dough. And yet… she wanted exactly what he described.

Her mug trembled as she set it down. *He deserves the truth. He deserves to know. But if I tell him or if he learns that the spell bent his heart even slightly will he look at me with the same tenderness? Or will I lose this too?*

Evander's gaze met hers unguarded now and stripped bare in a way that made her breath hitch. "That's why I come here Morgana. This place—" He gestured around at the quiet bakery, the shelves still dusted with flour. "It feels like that alley all over again. Like safety. Only this time… I don't have to hide. And you—"

He broke off, his jaw tightening as if the words pressed too hard against him.

Don't say it. Don't say it because if you do I'll want to believe it's real. And maybe it is, maybe it isn't, and the doubt will eat me alive.

She forced her lips into a careful smile. "I'm glad it feels safe here," she murmured.

But Evander only studied her. His eyes searched her face as though he knew she was deflecting. Then he set his mug aside and reached across the table. His hand brushed hers. They felt light at first then became firmer when she didn't pull away.

Morgana's breath caught.

The warmth of his palm spread up her arm straight to her chest and then curled around the ache that lived there. She wanted to sink into it and to let it mend the loneliness that had haunted her since her family's deaths since the moment she had chosen secrecy over honesty.

But the guilt was louder. *This is wrong. You're using him. You've been using him all along. Even if the spell only amplified what was already there you still interfered. You still tipped the scales.*

"Morgana," he said softly with her name like a vow on his lips. "I don't know if you realize what you've given me. But it's more than bread. More than sugar. It's… peace. And I don't take that for granted."

Her throat burned. Tears pricked her eyes before she could stop them. She ducked her head quickly, pretending to fuss with her mug and then praying that he wouldn't see.

He trusts me. He sees me as safety. And if he knew the truth that safety would shatter in his hands.

"I'm not... what you think I am," she whispered before she could stop herself.

Evander tilted his head. "What do you mean?"

Panic flared in her chest. "I just mean I'm no saint. I make mistakes. I get things wrong."

His expression softened. "So do I."

The simplicity of the answer unraveled her. He didn't press and didn't demand confessions. He just held her hand steady and warm as though to anchor her in place.

Her heart ached with longing. To tell him everything. To lay her secret bare and let him decide whether to stay or leave. But fear sealed her lips.

She squeezed his hand once gently then slipped hers free, retreating into the safety of her own lap. "You should finish your coffee," she said with her voice faint.

He didn't argue. But he didn't look away either. His eyes lingered on her filled with something so tender it left her breathless.

When he finally sipped from his mug again the silence between them was thick but not uncomfortable. It hummed with things unsaid and things that pressed at the edges of her chest until she thought she might break.

One day I'll tell him. I have to. But not tonight. Not when the wounds he shared are still raw. He deserves peace not more burdens.

She watched him memorizing the soft light on his face, the curve of his smile when he caught her looking, the boy he once was and the man he had become. And in the quiet of that moment Morgana realized something she had long tried to deny.

She was falling for him. Not the spell. Not the sweetness of a charm gone astray. For *him*.

And that truth was both the most beautiful and the most terrifying thing she had ever known.

Chapter 22 - Tension Peaks

The evening air inside *The Golden Spoon* was warm with the scent of cooling bread, sweet rolls, and cinnamon dust lingering faintly in the rafters. The last of the lanterns flickered against the walls their golden light settling like drowsy fireflies across the countertops. Morgana stacked pans mechanically with her hands moving with practiced ease though her mind spun restlessly. She had been trying for days to steady the chaos inside her chest. She had wanted to convince herself that Evander's smiles, his watchful concern, and his laughter that filled the bakery in ways brighter than any spell were his own. Yet even now her conscience gnawed like an insistent rat at the edges of every tender moment.

Evander reclined slightly against the counter with his arms folded firmly and watching her with that familiar intensity that never failed to make her pulse skip. His presence was like the hum of a storm too close to ignore. It was silent but electric. He hadn't said much tonight. Instead he lingered as if reluctant to leave. His eyes followed her movements as though afraid she might vanish the moment he turned away.

Finally he broke the silence. "You work too hard," he said softly. It was almost an accusation though softened by a smile. "Even after everyone's gone you don't stop."

Morgana glanced at him trying to keep her voice steady. "Bakeries don't run themselves."

"Maybe not," he admitted pushing away from the counter. His boots scuffed lightly on the worn wooden floor. "But sometimes I think you hide behind it. Like you'd rather bury yourself in flour than let someone help."

Her chest tightened. *If only you knew the truth, Evander.* She forced a light laugh. "It's better than letting the muffins burn."

He shook his head and stepped closer. It was so close that she could smell the faint trace of cedar and smoke clinging to him. She had come to crave that scent. His eyes softened, but there was something else there too. There was something taut beneath the surface. "Morgana you make it hard for a man to stand back." His voice dipped low and rough with emotion. "I keep telling myself not to hover not to care so much, but damn it I can't help it."

Her heart thudded painfully as she felt her palms dampening against the tray she held. The spell whispered like invisible threads tugging between them amplifying every word and every look. *Is this you Evander? Or is it me meddling with fate?*

Before she could answer and before she could even breathe properly he suddenly moved. One hand reached up. It felt gentle but firm as it brushed away a stray curl from her face. His thumb lingered at her cheek and his gaze burned into hers. Then in a rush he kissed her.

The world seemed to collapse in that instant. All she could feel was the warmth of his mouth against hers, the sudden rush of heat that surged through her body, and the trembling weakness in her knees. His hand slid to the back of her neck anchoring her head and pulling her against him as though he'd been waiting years and not weeks to do so. Morgana melted instinctively as her lips parted under his with a soft helpless sound.

The kiss was fierce but tender. It was unpolished and raw with need. For a heartbeat she forgot everything. Her guilt, her secrets, the spell that twisted around them like unseen vines. All she knew was him, the taste of him, the way his heartbeat thundered against her chest in perfect rhythm with her own.

But then reality stabbed through her haze of longing. *No. No this isn't fair. What if this isn't really his choice? What if it's the spell tightening its grip?* Guilt surged like ice water down her spine. She tore her lips away breathless. Her hand gently pressed against his chest to create space between them.

"Evander wait!" Her voice shook. She was caught between desperation and regret. "You shouldn't…"

Confusion flickered across his face. He appeared wounded and vulnerable though his hand still lingered at her arm. "I thought—" He swallowed, his voice rough. "Morgana I've wanted to do that since the first time you laughed at something I said. I thought you wanted it too."

Her throat closed. "I do," she whispered unable to lie. "More than you know. But I can't be sure it's you wanting this. Not completely."

His brows knit together as she saw frustration and tenderness mingling in his expression. "What do you mean?"

She couldn't tell him. Not yet. The words stuck in her throat heavy as stones. She lowered her gaze feeling her chest aching with the weight of her silence. *If I tell you will you walk away? Or will you look at me as if I've broken something fragile between us?*

Instead she shook her head. "I just… I don't want to take something that isn't freely given."

Evander's hand tightened briefly then fell away though he didn't retreat. His voice softened tentatively. "Morgana nothing about this is forced. I know what I feel."

Her heart twisted painfully. She wanted so badly to believe him, to lose herself in the warmth of his kiss again, to stop questioning every beat of affection he showed her. But the fear lingered sharp and unyielding. *The spell amplifies but doesn't create*, she reminded herself though the truth was a double-edged sword. That meant some part of his feelings were real, but how much? And could she ever know for certain?

Silence stretched between them filled only by the faint ticking of the cooling ovens. Morgana wrapped her arms around herself both to still her trembling and to fill the emptiness where his warmth had just been. Evander stood a pace away now with his shoulders tense and jaw set. The moment's fragile magic had shattered leaving only the echo of what might have been.

"I'm sorry," she whispered, her voice nearly breaking. "I just... I can't."

Evander looked at her for a long moment with his expression unreadable before finally nodding. "Then I'll wait," he said simply as his voice was rough but steady sounding. "For as long as it takes."

The quiet conviction in his words pierced her deeper than the kiss itself. *You deserve the truth*, she thought with tears stinging her eyes. *But how can I give it when it might destroy everything?*

Chapter 23 - The Confession Plan

Throughout the day the bakery had its usual regular customers come in. One of these customers was a longtime constable for the city. He had over 30 years of experience and was known for being very kind and approachable. As he bought his usual fruit tart Morgana engaged him in seemingly casual conversation.

She smiled at him. "Officer Pembert can I ask you a question for my own curiosity?"

He was visibly happy to talk with her. "Of course! Ask away!"

"Well as an officer of the law you must be well informed. You know that I'm just a simple witch, but it always pays to be well informed. What exactly would happen to someone who used magic in food?"

Alden Pembert smiled kindly at her in response. "Right you are to always be well informed. It's a serious matter. Along with a member of the constabulary a representative of the Provincial Magistrate would visit the accused. There would eventually be a public trial and if the person is found guilty then they would lose their work license, be imprisoned in the royal jails, face a hefty fine, and probably be publicly scorned by the community members."

"Thank you so much Officer Pembert. I was so morbidly curious about it."

"Of course Morgana! Always happy to help especially when you make such delicious baked goods." He chuckled lightly.

After waiting on some more customers throughout the day Morgana got her usual lull in the evening. It was a steady stream of customers, but nothing she couldn't handle.

The bakery was quiet though the silence was not the peaceful kind. It weighed on Morgana's shoulders thick and pressing as if every shadow clung too tightly to the corners. The ovens had long since cooled. The air was stripped of its cozy hum leaving only the faint sweetness of sugar and a lingering bitterness she could not shake. Morgana sat at one of the small wooden tables, the kind meant for customers who lingered with their tea. Her elbows were braced against the grain and her head was resting in her hands.

Her lips still tingled with memory. The kiss. It haunted her. No matter how many trays she scrubbed or how many cupboards she rearranged her memory of it returned warm and unbidden. It tugged at the very place she had tried so hard to shield. It had felt like truth, but the truth she feared most was that it might not have been his alone to give.

It's not enough anymore, she told herself as she squeezed her hands together until her knuckles ached. *I can't keep dancing around this. He deserves the truth. Even if it ruins everything.*

She thought of her mother, of the evenings when flour dusted their hair like winter snow, of the lessons whispered in the hush of twilight while the ovens burned low. *Magic is a gift Morgana, but a dangerous one. It bends hearts as easily as dough if you're not careful. And hearts are not meant to be bent.* Her mother's voice lingered. It was so clear it nearly undid her. All of them were gone now. Her father, mother, and siblings were all claimed by time and tragedy. She alone carried the burden of memory and with it the lessons she had sworn not to betray. Yet here she was trembling beneath the weight of having already betrayed them.

Morgana straightened slowly drawing a sharp breath. "I'll tell him," she whispered aloud as the words startled her in the empty shop. The lanterns flickered against the glass as if in answer. "I'll tell him everything."

The thought alone made her stomach twist. What if he looked at her with horror? What if the softness in his gaze hardened into something cold and final? What if his laughter that warm disarming sound she had come to lean on never again rose inside these walls?

But there was another truth too. It was quieter but still undeniable. What if he understood? What if he had already seen enough of her to know that she had not meant to trap him? That the girl who brewed magic into baked goods was the same girl who blushed at his smiles and worried over his tea?

The risk burned, but so did the hope.

She rose from the chair and paced feeling her apron strings brushing against her skirt. She needed a plan. Simply blurting out a confession would shatter them both. She would need to choose the moment carefully. It would have to be a time when Evander's temper was steady and when the air wasn't thick with exhaustion or distraction. He had shared so much of himself in recent days. He told her his regrets, his stories, and the tender pieces he didn't let others see. He deserved the same honesty from her no matter how it ended.

But what if waiting only makes it worse? she thought, gripping the edge of the counter until her fingers stung. *Every day I wait the spell lingers. Every smile and every glance… what if it grows stronger? What if I'm already too late?*

Her breath shuddered. She closed her eyes, forcing herself to picture his face when she spoke the words: *Evander I used magic on the cookies. I didn't mean for it to touch you, but it did. Would his jaw tighten? Would he step back with hurt radiating like cracks in glass? Or would he lean closer asking questions and trying to understand?*

"I can't keep guessing," she muttered. "I need to know."

Her heart tugged at her in two directions. They were the longing to cling to what they had however fragile and the resolve to stand by the truth even if it shattered into dust. She had spent so much of her life hiding: her magic, her grief, the cracks in her heart left by losing everyone she had loved. She had tucked it all away beneath a smile and beneath sugar and butter and warm bread. But hiding had only brought her here, teetering on the edge of losing the one thing she wanted most.

No more hiding.

She moved into the kitchen. The space was her familiar sanctuary of polished wood and iron. The counters were bare and the shelves orderly yet she touched them as though they could offer courage. She had learned long ago that recipes were easier to follow than feelings. The steps were clear and precise while the outcomes were predictable. But there was no recipe for this. Only her own trembling courage that was measured imperfectly with no guarantee of sweetness at the end.

The night deepened. She lit a single lantern by the window. Its glow spilled out from the bakery onto the cobblestones outside. The quiet felt heavier with each passing minute as anticipation built inside her chest like the rising of dough. Tomorrow. She would tell him tomorrow before another day could knot her resolve.

Mother give me strength, she thought looking up into the dim rafters. *Father remind me of honor. Brothers and sisters stand with me when I speak.* The silence gave no answer, but the memories pressed close and warmed her like unseen arms.

For the first time in weeks her decision felt like a steady flame instead of a flickering wick. She would tell him. She would lay bare the truth no matter how it hurt. If he walked away at least it would be real. And if by some miracle he stayed then perhaps they could begin again this time on ground untwisted by magic.

Her throat tightened as she whispered into the empty bakery, "Please let him see me. Just me."

The lantern flame swayed casting her shadow tall and trembling against the wall. Tomorrow she would speak. Tonight she would hold onto that fragile ember of resolve and guard it as though it were the most precious spell she had ever woven.

Chapter 24 – Mistaken Timing

Morgana woke with a resolve so sharp it almost hurt. Today she would tell him. The secret had eaten at her long enough after nights of turning over every possible outcome from rejection, disgust, maybe even understanding. She could no longer stomach the thought of living half in a lie. She would confess. No more delays.

She rehearsed the words as she tied her apron that morning. Each knot tugged with grim determination. *Evander I used magic in the bakery. It touched you when it never should have. I never meant for it to happen, but it did. And you deserve the truth.* Simple and direct. He might hate her for it, but he would at least hate her honestly.

The Golden Spoon smelled sweet and steady, but the familiar comforts did little to soothe the nervous fire twisting in her stomach. The ovens hummed, bread browned, pastries puffed in tidy rows. Everything was perfectly ordinary. For once she wished it would stay that way.

But magic never seemed to grant her that wish.

It began subtly the way it always did. There was a faint vibration in the air like static before a storm. She was glazing a tray of cinnamon rolls when the spoon in her hand gave a twitch slipping from her grip and flicking glaze in a neat arc across her cheek. Morgana froze.

Not today. Please not today.

The spoon quivered again then shot into the bowl of glaze like it had a will of its own. The glaze bubbled unnaturally frothing higher and higher until it spilled over the rim. She snatched for it muttering a counter-word under her breath, but the spell rippled outward. A stack of eclairs on the cooling rack gave a sudden wiggle then began inching across the counter like determined caterpillars.

"Oh no," Morgana whispered. "Not the pastries—"

One cream puff launched straight into the air with a pop, smacking the cupboard before tumbling back down. Another bounced like a rubber ball ricocheting off the wall and narrowly missing her head. Morgana lunged to grab it, but in the process knocked the tray of eclairs to the floor where they wriggled indignantly as though trying to escape.

Her heart plummeted.

The bell above the bakery door jingled.

"Morgana?" Evander's voice carried through the front.

Her eyes widened in horror. *Not now, not now, not—*

He stepped into the kitchen doorway just in time to see a cream puff sail gracefully through the air and splat against the far wall. Morgana stood in the middle of the chaos, flour on her face, glaze dripping from her sleeve, eclairs wriggling around her boots like caught fish.

His eyebrows shot up. "What in the world…?"

"I—it's nothing!" she stammered, snatching two eclairs and shoving them back onto the counter. They immediately flipped themselves onto their sides and flopped off again.

Evander blinked then of all things he laughed. It was a warm incredulous sound that made her cheeks burn. "Are you at war with the pastries?"

"They started it," Morgana muttered under her breath, lunging for a rogue cream puff that had rolled beneath the table.

Evander stepped forward grinning as though he'd stumbled into some grand comedy rather than a disaster. "Here let me." He reached for one of the bouncing puffs only to have it burst open in his hand and spray cream all over his tunic. He stopped blinking down at the mess then laughed again as he shook his head.

Morgana wanted the floor to swallow her whole. She'd been preparing to bare her soul to him and instead he was standing there dripping custard while enchanted pastries staged a rebellion around them.

The chaos only escalated. A fruit tart shimmied to the edge of a shelf and leapt like a lemming, splattering berries across the floor. The cake she'd painstakingly layered that morning began to wobble violently and then teetered as though drunk before collapsing with a dramatic splat onto the counter. Morgana tried to save it, but her sleeve caught in the bowl of glaze sending the spoon clattering to the floor where it spun like a top.

Evander bent to retrieve it still smiling and utterly oblivious to the crushing despair tightening in her chest. "You really do push yourself too hard Morgana," he said softly as though the mess were only a sign of exhaustion and not a magical catastrophe. "You don't have to do all of this alone."

Her throat closed. *That's not what this is. This isn't tiredness. This is me. This is my fault.*

But she couldn't speak the words. Not with sugar sliding down the cupboards and dough balls thumping against the table legs. Not with him looking at her like she was simply overworked like all she needed was rest. If she confessed now with custard still dripping down his tunic he'd think she was raving from fatigue. The moment she had built herself up for was destroyed by pastries.

She grabbed another cream puff before it could roll under the stove, holding it like a prisoner. "I—I had meant to." She faltered. The words *tell you the truth* clawed at her tongue, but they would not come. Not with his smile soft and amused and not with the kitchen mocking her resolve.

Evander reached out to brush a smear of glaze from her cheek with his thumb. "See? You're covered in proof. You need rest Morgana. Not endless work. You can lean on me sometimes."

Her breath hitched. He thought she was tired. He thought this was just a baker's clumsiness. He thought he was helping. And she was failing him again and letting the truth sink deeper into shadows.

It was supposed to be today.

The last cream puff gave one final heroic bounce and exploded against the wall. Evander chuckled, shaking his head as though it were all some harmless joke. But Morgana could only feel the crushing weight of her frustration, embarrassment, and the certainty that the spell would not wait forever.

Not today, she thought bitterly clutching the ruined pastry in her hands. *But soon. Before it's too late.*

Chapter 25 – Heartfelt Discussion

The bakery was quiet in the late afternoon with the hum of the ovens fading after the rush of customers had passed. A soft golden light streamed through the front windows catching motes of flour dust still lingering in the air. Morgana leaned against the counter, wiping her hands on her apron though they were already clean. Her mind was restless and her heart pounding in her chest like an overzealous drummer. The air smelled of caramelized sugar and coffee grounds. It was usually warm and inviting yet she felt no comfort in it now.

Today had to be the day. She had put it off long enough. Every moment of laughter, every accidental brush of Evander's hand against hers, every kind smile that softened the weariness in his eyes was drowning her. It all burned brighter with the weight of her guilt. She had admitted once in passing that she had "messed up a spell." But she had hidden the heart of it and the truth that their closeness was entangled with something that had never been meant to happen. She couldn't let this continue without honesty. Not anymore.

Evander came through from the storeroom then rolling his shoulders as if easing off tension and carrying a sack of sugar over one arm like it weighed nothing. He set it down with a casual grunt, brushing his palms together, and smiled at her. That smile made her knees weak though she hated herself for wondering. *How much of that warmth is truly his? How much is mine to claim?*

"You've been awfully quiet," Evander remarked to her as he casually leaned his hip against the counter. "Not like you Morgana. Usually by this point in the day you've already scolded me at least once for stacking trays wrong or drinking too much of the leftover coffee."

She tried to laugh but it came out brittle. "Maybe I'm saving all my scolding for later."

He chuckled. His voice sounded low and easy. The sound twisted uncomfortably in her chest.

Tell him now. Just say it.

But the words stuck. They were as sticky as honey in her throat.

Instead she said, "Do you ever get tired of it? The bakery I mean. The routine of it all?"

Evander tilted his head, considering. "Tired? No. Worn out sure. But I like it here. It feels… I don't know maybe steady. Like if the world outside crumbled there'd still be bread rising and cookies cooling on racks. It's a sort of anchor."

Her stomach turned. The bakery was his anchor, and she had infected it with secrets. "Evander can we—can we talk? Properly?"

He straightened up. His expression sharpened at her tone. "Talk? That sounds serious."

"It is."

For a moment silence stretched between them. It was taut and unsteady. He gestured toward one of the little tables by the window where customers usually lingered with pastries and coffee. "All right. Let's sit then."

Morgana's hands trembled as she untied her apron and draped it over the counter. She sat opposite him, staring at the worn wood of the tabletop and tracing one of the little knife grooves with her fingertip. Words wanted to spill out, but where to begin? How to untangle weeks of quiet deceit?

Evander leaned forward resting his forearms on the table. "You're scaring me a little you know. You look like you're about to tell me someone died."

Her throat closed. *They did. Everyone did. My family. My mother, my father, my siblings. But that isn't what you need to know. That's not the first thing.*

"No one died," she whispered. "At least not recently."

He frowned with his brows knitting, but he didn't interrupt.

Morgana took a breath so deep it hurt. "I need to tell you something about myself. About… what I've done."

He sat back waiting. His patience felt unnerving.

"You know how I said once that I 'messed up a spell'? That wasn't the whole truth." Her fingers twisted together in her lap. "I've always had magic. It runs in my bloodline. My mother taught me to use it carefully and wisely. She told me it wasn't meant for selfishness or shortcuts. And I thought I understood her. But when I came here, when I started baking in this town, I got careless. No I got greedy."

Evander's eyes widened slightly, but he said nothing only listening.

"I was lonely," Morgana admitted to him. The words tumbled out faster now as though once begun they could not be stopped. "I wanted people to love my baking and to love this place. So I started weaving small enchantments into the dough. They were just small charms for warmth, for happiness, for comfort.

Nothing harmful I thought. Just… a nudge. A way to make people come back. But then I tried something more complicated. A binding spell. It was supposed to be harmless. Just a test." Her voice broke. "And it pulled you to me."

Evander blinked. "Pulled me?"

"Yes." Her eyes burned with tears she didn't dare shed. "That's why you started spending so much time here. Why you… why you cared. Or at least, why I thought you did. The spell tangled with your feelings. It didn't create them, but it *amplified* them. It made you feel things stronger than you might have otherwise. And I hated myself for it even as I—" She cut her words off, pressing a hand over her mouth.

The silence that followed was unbearable.

Evander leaned back in his chair with his gaze fixed on her with an intensity that made her want to flee. Finally he said slowly, "You're telling me… you enchanted me? That all this time my choices weren't really mine?"

Her heart cracked. "I don't know. That's what terrifies me. I never wanted to control you Evander. Not you. I kept trying to undo if and to hopefully fix it, but magic has its own stubbornness. And every time you smiled at me and every time you laughed I wondered if it was because you wanted to… or because I'd stolen your choice."

He was quiet for so long she thought she might shatter into a thousand shards on the spot. Then he exhaled and leaned forward again with his elbows on the table and his hands clasped.

"You could have kept this from me," he said. "Why tell me now?"

"Because I can't bear it anymore," Morgana whispered. "Because I look at you and I-" She broke off unable to finish. *Because I love you. And love built on a lie is no love at all.*

Evander studied her with his brow furrowed in thought. There was no anger in his face. At least not the kind of anger that she had braced for. Instead there was a kind of stunned and cautious curiosity like a man trying to piece together a puzzle missing half its edges.

"So," he said carefully, "magic is real. You have it. You've been using it in your baking. And somehow that spilled over into me."

"Yes."

"And you're telling me all this because you want... what? Forgiveness?"

"No." She shook her head, tears finally slipping down her cheeks. "Not forgiveness. I don't deserve that. I just want you to know. I want you to have the truth even if it means you walk away. You deserve to make your own choice."

Evander's lips pressed into a thin line. He sat back with his gaze flicking toward the racks of cooling bread behind the counter then back to her. "I should feel furious," he admitted. "I should storm out, call you a manipulator, never come back. But—" He let out a short laugh. It sounded slightly incredulous. "Instead I'm thinking about how absurd it sounds. About how if you'd told me on my first day here that you bake magic into cookies I'd have thought you'd lost your mind. But now? Now it feels like the only thing that makes sense of... everything."

Her breath caught. "You're not angry?"

"Oh I'm unsettled," he said running a hand through his hair. "Confused. A little betrayed yes. But also strangely fascinated." His eyes softened. "You're telling me the truth now. That matters more than you think."

Morgana's chest ached with the force of her relief though guilt still pressed heavy. "I'm so sorry Evander. I never wanted to take your freedom. I only wanted... I only wanted you to see me."

"I do see you," he said quietly. "Magic or not. And I need time to think and to sort through this. But I'm not walking away. Not yet."

The words wrapped around her like a fragile gift she dared not hold too tightly. Her tears fell freely now and she let them. For the first time in months the air felt clearer and the burden of secrecy lifting. She didn't know what the future would hold and whether forgiveness would ever truly come, but for the first time hope glimmered among the ruins of fear.

And Evander though shaken didn't leave the table. He stayed there and leaned forward with curiosity flickering in his gaze like the light of a candle that refused to be snuffed out.

The silence that followed felt too large for the small room like a loaf left to rise too long. Evander's face was steady but something in his jaw worked tight.

"I don't know what's mine anymore," he said at last with the words sounding low and careful. "Every look and every thought I can't tell if it's me... or your spell."

Morgana's fingers went cold on her apron. "I never meant to take anything from you." Her voice broke on the last word. She wanted to reach for him, but instead she folded her hands as if to show she wouldn't hold him against his will.

He lifted a hand. It wasn't done harshly, but only to keep the distance she'd offered. "You can't undo that truth for me," he said. "Not all at once."

"Then tell me what you need," she whispered. "If stepping back is how you find out then I'll do it."

Evander closed his eyes breathing out slow. When he opened them his expression was softer but guarded. "Give me time. If the spell fades and I still want this then I'll know it's mine."

Chapter 26 – Processing Truth

Evander barely slept that night. He lay on his narrow bed in the small room he was renting and staring at the ceiling as shadows shifted with the passing moonlight, listening to the faint creaks of the old timbers. The words Morgana had spoken repeated themselves in endless circles. *I cast a spell. I pulled you to me. The feelings you have are amplified and not born of your own choosing.* Each phrase struck against the walls of his mind like pebbles tossed at glass each one making another crack in what he thought he knew of himself.

He had always trusted the solidity of his own choices. Work hard, earn your keep, live simply. That was the way he'd shaped his life. To learn that some unseen force had taken hold of him, tangled his emotions, bent them toward someone else, and left him with the dizzying feeling of standing on ground that had turned to water. *What part of me is real?* he wondered. *What part is borrowed? Or worse yet stolen?* The questions gnawed at him sharp as a blade dragged across his thoughts.

Yet when he thought of Morgana's face that was pale with guilt as she confessed and her voice trembling with tears shining in her eyes he couldn't summon hatred. Betrayal yes. Confusion that cut so deep it nearly hollowed him. But hatred? No. Because even now in the wake of her honesty he still wanted to be near her. The very fact made him want to laugh bitter and bewildered. Even with his certainty shattered he still wanted to be near her. He practically yearned for it.

He rolled onto his side clutching the pillow. *Is that the spell talking or me?*

Morning came too quickly. He forced himself up, dragging his shirt over his head and rubbing the weariness from his face. He

167

decided that he would still visit the bakery like normal though this time he felt some trepidation. A part of him ached for the simple comfort of her presence. He yearned for the warmth he had once taken as real. But now every flicker of desire was tangled with suspicion. *Was it truly his own or just the echo of magic she had woven around him?* The longing remained feeling sharp and insistent yet it was also laced with a feeling of bitterness that he could not shake right now.

Morgana was already bustling and moving trays of rolls from the ovens. The sweet scent of cinnamon sugar filled the air. She glanced up as he entered and her hands faltered for just a breath before she turned back to her work. Her hair had come loose from its braid with strands curling at her temples. She didn't try to speak and neither did he.

The silence between them was thick and almost solid. He helped with the bread, wiped down counters, and arranged pastries in the display. Every so often his gaze would catch on her profile and his chest would squeeze. *She's a liar*, part of him whispered. *She stole your choice.* But another part argued just as fiercely. *She told you the truth when she didn't have to. She could have hidden it forever.*

By midday he couldn't take it anymore. He stepped outside with a cloth slung over his shoulder gulping down the crisp autumn air. The bustle of the marketplace stretched around him. Voices rose in chatter and horses clopped past with their heavy steps echoing on the cobblestones. People waved to him. He was known now as the tall man who worked with the mysterious baker. He managed a nod, but his stomach churned.

He walked away from the square down quieter streets lined with leaning wooden houses and vines climbing up window frames. Finally he stopped at the edge of the river where the old stone bridge arched over the water. He leaned against the railing, staring at the current sweeping leaves downstream.

What do I feel? he asked himself as his fingers tightened on the cool stone. *Strip away the magic and what's left?*

He thought back to the first day he had walked into *The Golden Spoon* seeking nothing more than a place to sit and rest. The moment she had looked at him he had felt something then. A spark of curiosity and maybe of comfort even though he had brushed it aside. *Was that spellwork or had it been there from the start?*

He remembered the long evenings when Morgana stayed behind testing recipes, brow furrowed in concentration, and with flour streaking her cheek. He had wanted to laugh, to brush it away, to see her smile. He had wanted to know her stories, her thoughts, her dreams. He had felt protective of her yes. Perhaps he was too protective at times. But was that entirely unnatural? He had lost enough in his own life to understand the ache of loneliness in another.

He exhaled, closing his eyes. *So much of it feels real. Too real to be only magic.*

Still doubt gnawed at him. *What if those tender stirrings and those quickened heartbeats weren't his at all? What if he was just a puppet dancing on invisible strings woven into dough and sugar?*

A voice from memory came to him then unbidden. He thought about his grandmother's voice. It always sounded stern but kind. "The heart is stubborn boy. You can't make it love where it does not wish to love. You can coax and you can cajole, but in the end it always chooses." She had said it to him when he was a teenager and was heartbroken for the first time. He had scoffed then. He was too young to believe wisdom could ease pain. But now the words struck deep.

Could it be true? That Morgana's spell had merely magnified what was already there? That the seed of it had always been his own?

The thought twisted through him like a blade turned sideways. Part of him wanted to believe it. That his heart had chosen her long before magic muddied the truth. But doubt shadowed every tender memory. *Was her laughter a sound he loved or one the spell had coaxed him to crave? Was the steadiness he found in her company created by his own longing or something stitched into him without his consent?* The more he searched himself the less certain he became. He felt caught between the ache of wanting her and the bitter suspicion that even his desire was not entirely his.

He stayed by the river until the sun dipped lower and its light turned amber on the rippling surface. Only then did he turn back toward the bakery feeling no closer to answers yet unwilling to stay away.

When he returned the shop was quiet again and the last of the customers were gone. Morgana was wiping down tables. Her movements were precise, but her shoulders were hunched over as though bracing for whatever might come. She looked up when he entered. Her expression was guarded but also hopeful looking. "You're back," she said softly.

"Of course I came back," he replied though his voice sounded rough in his own ears. He hesitated then added, "I needed space to think."

She nodded setting the cloth aside. "And... did you?"

"Yes. And no." He crossed to the counter, leaning against it and staring down at the wood. "I can't untangle what's mine and what isn't. I can't just snap my fingers and know which feelings are real. But I also can't deny that I care for you. I don't know how much of that is me and how much is the spell, but it's there. It's strong. And I don't think I can just pretend it isn't."

Her lips parted. A faint tremor ran through her hands at his words. "Evander..."

"I'm not saying it fixes everything," he interrupted. "I'm not saying I trust you fully yet. I need time. I need honesty. If we're to have anything at all then you can't hide from me again."

Her throat tightened, but she forced the words past it. "I know I've broken something precious," she whispered as her voice trembled like thin glass. "I can't undo what I did, but I can choose differently now. No more secrets, no more spells, no more pretending it was easier to lie than to face the truth. If you'll let me I'll give you all of me both the good and the flawed because you deserve nothing less than the truth. I don't want to lose what we still might have."

He looked at her then. He really looked. The weariness in her eyes, the hope trembling beneath fear, the woman who had made mistakes but had bared her soul rather than continue the lie.

And though his chest was still full of turmoil it was also filled with a fragile thread of something else that wove through it. It was something like possibility.

He exhaled slowly, pushing away from the counter. "I'm going back to my room for now. I need rest. But Morgana—" His voice softened surprising even himself. "Don't be afraid I'll vanish. I'm still here."

Her eyes shone though she said nothing and only nodded.

When he climbed the stairs and closed the door behind him Evander rested against it and dragged a calloused hand over his face. He was still confused, still unsure, still searching himself for clarity. But one truth pulsed steady beneath the noise: he wanted to stay. And maybe in time he would know why.

Chapter 27 – Rebuilding Trust

The days that followed were quiet, but not in the comfortable way they had once been. Silence lingered between them. It wasn't sharp like a blade but tender and raw like the silence of two people relearning how to stand near one another. Morgana felt it with every step she took through the bakery, every tray she lifted, and every glance she dared send in Evander's direction. It was not the silence of anger she told herself. It was the silence of rebuilding.

She had expected distance after her confession. Maybe cold shoulders, clipped words, and perhaps even his leaving altogether. But Evander had not left. That fact alone felt like sunlight breaking through storm clouds. He stayed. He worked. He spoke when there was need to speak and answered when she asked. And though the warmth that once came so easily between them was dulled it had not vanished entirely.

Morgana decided then that words alone would not be enough. Trust was not built in a single moment of honesty. It was built in the quiet things like the acts of care that asked for nothing in return. If he could see day by day that she meant what she said that she wanted him free and not bound then perhaps the cracks between them could mend.

The first morning she rose earlier than usual and slipped downstairs while the stars still glimmered faintly above the rooftops. She kneaded the dough herself, working it until her arms ached and humming a tune her mother used to sing. The ovens glowed warmly by the time Evander appeared rubbing sleep from his eyes. He blinked when he saw her already pulling the first loaves free.

"You've done all this yourself?" he asked as surprise softened the roughness of his morning voice.

Morgana brushed a stray hair from her face and nodded. "I thought you might like a slower morning. Less rushing. More coffee." She set a steaming cup on the counter for him. It was dark and rich the way he preferred with the faintest hint of cinnamon stirred in.

He hesitated then accepted it with his fingers brushing the rim. "Thank you. I appreciate the thought."

It was only a few words, but they carried weight. He sipped and for a moment his shoulders eased. Morgana caught the flicker of relief in his expression and her chest loosened just a little.

That became her pattern. Small things and careful things. She mended the hem of his sleeve when it caught on a nail, leaving the stitches neat and tidy. She set aside the last honey roll for him when customers had devoured the rest. She made sure to ask about his back when he lifted heavy flour sacks. And then she pressed a hot cloth into his hands when he admitted to a twinge. Never pressing too far and never demanding thanks. She simply was offering what she could.

And slowly she noticed his walls soften.

One afternoon after the last customer left Evander lingered at the counter while she swept. He reclined against the wood casually. His arms were folded together and he watched her closely with that steady gaze of his. "You're working yourself too hard again," he said.

She smiled faintly though her heart felt like 100 small hummingbirds beating their wings. "Maybe I am. But it feels different now."

"How so?"

"Because I'm not trying to hide behind it." She rested the broom meeting his eyes. "I don't want to drown myself in work and pretend everything is fine. I want to do the work and share it with you openly. Even the mistakes. Even the fears."

Something flickered across his face. At first she saw surprise and then thoughtfulness. He gave a small nod as though he was tucking her words away. The silence between them stretched. It wasn't heavy but it did feel fragile like a thread that could hold or break. When his gaze returned to her it carried the weight of someone testing the shape of trust. It was uncertain but unwilling to let it go entirely.

The next day it was he who made the coffee first, sliding a cup toward her with the faintest smile tugging at his lips. She accepted it with both hands. She felt a warmth spreading through her chest that had nothing to do with the drink.

It was in these little trades of care back and forth that something fragile began to grow again. Morgana did not let herself hope too fiercely, but she felt it as the thread of connection wove them tighter.

One evening after closing she lit a single candle at one of the back tables and brought out a small plate she had hidden away. It was two slices of honey cake drizzled lightly with a citrus glaze. "Sit with me?" she asked.

Evander raised an eyebrow but obeyed as he slowly pulled out the chair opposite her. The candle cast shadows across his face softening his strong features. The candlelight caught in his eyes and made them gleam with a warmth that contrasted the guarded set of his jaw.

"I made this with no charms," she said before he could ask. "Just sugar, flour, and a little patience. I wanted you to know that I can."

He picked up his fork cutting a bite carefully. His expression remained neutral as he tasted it, but then his brows lifted slightly. "It's good."

Relief fluttered in her chest. "Not as sweet as it might have been perhaps."

"It's enough," he said simply and for the first time in days his gaze lingered on her longer than necessary.

Morgana looked down quickly, heat rushing to her cheeks. *Don't mistake it*, she scolded herself. *Don't reach for more than what is here.* And yet in the quiet glow she couldn't help but feel the hope stirring again.

Trust she knew was not rebuilt in grand gestures. It was in letting him see her as she was. Unguarded, clumsy, even weak at times. So she did not hide the moments when her hands trembled, when memories of her family rose too sharp, when she burned a batch of rolls because her thoughts wandered. She let him see. And he in turn did not mock and did not scold. He simply watched and sometimes when she least expected it he offered his presence like a hand resting near hers. Not quite touching, but there.

It was enough to keep her steady.

One night she found herself alone in the bakery long after Evander had gone to his room. She sat at a table with her mother's old recipe book open and the ink faded on the pages. Her eyes lingered on a note in the margin that was written in her mother's looping hand. *A good baker puts love into the dough not spells. The bread will carry it farther than magic ever could.*

Morgana's throat tightened. She traced the words with her fingertip blinking back tears. *I'm trying Mama. I'm trying to do it right this time.*

A creak on the old wooden floor startled her and she looked up to see Evander lingering at the threshold. He must have come to the bakery for a late night craving for something sweet, but he paused when he saw her with the book. "Couldn't sleep?" he asked.

"No," she admitted. Her voice sounded small.

He approached glancing at the page. "That's hers?"

Morgana nodded. "The only thing I still have of her. Sometimes I wonder if I've betrayed her with the way I've used magic. She believed in honesty and in care. In bread that was just bread."

Evander was quiet for a long moment then said, "You told me the truth. That matters. It doesn't erase what happened, but it matters."

She looked at him as the weight of those words pressed a warmth into her chest. She swallowed hard. "Do you think you'll ever forgive me?"

His gaze was steady and searching. "I think I'm already trying."

Her breath caught. Relief and longing tangled in her ribs. She lowered her eyes not trusting herself to speak without breaking.

They stood there in the candlelight the quiet between them was no longer sharp and no longer painful. It was soft now like dough resting before it rose. It was patient and full of possibility.

Morgana thought of the silence as a promise. It was fragile yes, but alive.

Chapter 28 – Baking Together

The morning broke with soft light spilling into the bakery. Golden rays painted the wooden beams overhead. Dust motes drifted lazily in the sunbeams and glittered like enchanted sparks as Morgana pushed open the shutters. The familiar warmth of *The Golden Spoon* wrapped around her. She could easily detect the mingled scents of sugar, butter, and fresh bread rising from the ovens as though the walls themselves breathed with her work.

She pulled her hair into a messy knot as her sleeves were rolled up high and then she set a bowl on the counter. Flour hissed into it. The white plume curled like smoke before settling. The simple rhythm of baking soothed her in ways little else could. This time though the flour wasn't entirely obedient. It gave a soft *poof* as if sighing at her and rose in a friendly cloud before returning itself neatly to the bowl.

Morgana laughed lightly under her breath. *At least it's playful now instead of rebellious.*

"Should I be worried that your ingredients have taken on a life of their own?"

She turned at the sound of his voice. Evander stood in the doorway. His hair was still damp from washing up and the morning light caught the strong line of his jaw. His brows lifted in amusement as he took in the flour cloud drifting between them.

Morgana shrugged with a sheepish grin. "Not alive. Just…cooperative."

"Cooperative?" He stepped forward, trailing a finger across the flour-dusted counter. "I'm not sure that's the word I'd use." His lips quirked. "Enchanted maybe."

She gave him a look that was meant to be stern though her smile betrayed her. "If you're going to stand there and make clever remarks you might as well be useful. I'm testing a new recipe."

"Testing?" His tone was mock-serious. "I thought you already had enough sweets to supply the entire capital."

"Not like this." Morgana turned to the shelf and pulled down a small tin wrapped in a protective warding charm. She opened it carefully to reveal cinnamon. It was dark and fragrant. "Charmed cinnamon. Gentle, warm, nothing dangerous. It's supposed to enhance flavor and maybe bring a little comfort."

"And the mood?" he teased.

She rolled her eyes. "If it does that's incidental."

Evander's grin deepened, but he didn't press. He simply nodded at her with curiosity glinting in his eyes. She marveled at the ease of it. There were no shadows of doubt and no guarded distance. After everything he was still here.

"Right then," she said briskly. "Apron. Now."

"I don't wear aprons," he protested.

"You do today." She tossed him one and to her delight he actually tied it on though his expression suggested he was bracing for battle.

They began with eggs. Morgana cracked hers smoothly, but Evander's first attempt ended in disaster. There was shell shattered in his palm and yolk sliding down his fingers in sticky golden ribbons.

He grimaced. "This is more perilous than the sword."

Morgana nearly doubled over laughing. "You can't possibly compare an egg to combat."

"Can't I? At least on the battlefield no one expects elegance." He shook his sticky hand in frustration, spattering the counter with yolk.

"Stop! You'll ruin everything." She caught his wrist though she was laughing so hard she could barely breathe. "Oh gods you're hopeless."

He looked at her with mock offense then broke into a grin. "Hopelessly charming perhaps."

She swatted him with a towel, but her heart raced for reasons that had nothing to do with eggs.

They carried on though their rhythm was more chaos than order. Evander added too much flour, sneezed, and sent a cloud rising that coated them both from head to toe. Morgana's hair turned white with powder and Evander's dark tunic looked as though it had been snowed on. She tried to scold him but dissolved into laughter instead.

The magic seemed to approve of their merriment. A spoon began to stir itself lazily in a bowl of batter. A sugar jar tipped just enough to scatter glittering crystals across the counter. A whisk floated briefly before plopping back into the bowl with a splash.

Evander blinked at the antics then chuckled, low and genuine. "Your kitchen's alive Morgana. Should I be impressed or unsettled?"

"Both," she admitted. "But today it feels like it wants to play." She lifted her hand and coaxed the spoon into a graceful spin. The batter smoothed itself as though kneaded by invisible hands. "It never used to feel like this. Before it fought me. Now it's like the bakery knows me."

He watched her closely and his voice softened. "You look happy."

Her breath caught. She set the spoon down carefully. "I am. For the first time in a long while I don't feel like I'm hiding."

The words lingered between them and for once the silence was comfortable. Then perhaps unable to bear the weight of it Evander dipped a finger into the batter and licked it clean.

"Evander!" Morgana gasped. "That's raw!"

He licked his finger again grinning unrepentantly. "Worth it. Sweet as sin."

"You're impossible," she muttered trying to glare.

"And you adore me for it."

Her cheeks burned. She turned quickly back to the dough unwilling to let him see just how much truth he'd stumbled upon.

They worked side by side. Rolling, shaping, and braiding. Evander's attempt at braiding dough was a catastrophe. One lump of dough looked more like a knotted rope than a pastry.

Morgana laughed so hard she nearly dropped her own braid. "By the gods what is that?"

He inspected it solemnly. "A bold artistic choice."

"It looks like it was pulled from a fishing boat."

"Then perhaps I should stick to taste-testing," he said, eyes sparkling.

The oven warmed the room filling the air with the scent of cinnamon and butter. Morgana leaned against the counter breathing it in. Beside her Evander stood close enough that his shoulder brushed hers. For once she didn't pull away.

"You know," he said quietly, "I never thought I'd find peace in a kitchen. But this feels like home."

Her chest tightened. She smiled softly. "Then stay. As long as you like."

The oven timer rang saving her from her emotional tears. They pulled the trays out. The pastries were golden, steaming, and the tops were dusted with sugar that crackled as it cooled. Evander immediately reached for one.

"They're hot!" Morgana warned.

Too late. He yelped after the first bite, fanning his mouth with both hands. Morgana doubled over laughing so hard she had to clutch the counter for support.

"You laugh too much at my suffering," he accused once he'd cooled his mouth with a gulp of water.

"Only when you bring it upon yourself," she wheezed.

But when he finally took a proper bite his expression shifted to wonder. "Morgana this is incredible."

She tasted her own. The flavor was rich, warm, and comforting. It was just as she'd hoped. No false compulsion and no unnatural pull. Only cinnamon, butter, and sweetness.

"This," she whispered almost to herself, "is how it was always meant to be."

Evander looked at her and something unspoken passed between them. Not heat, not guilt, just trust.

The rest of the afternoon unfolded in laughter. They staged flour battles that left the floor dusted white, dropped a spoon only for it to bounce upright on its own, and decorated pastries with sugar swirls that shaped themselves into hearts and stars as if the kitchen itself wanted to join their game.

By evening trays upon trays lined the counters each pastry golden and gleaming. The bakery smelled heavenly. It was a delicious tapestry of spice and sweetness that drifted out the windows and drew curious passersby to linger at the door.

Evander leaned against the frame, surveying their work with pride. "I'd say we make a decent team."

Morgana who had cheeks sore from smiling wiped off some stray flour from her arms. "The best."

And for the first time she believed it with no secrets and no fear. Just flour, sugar, laughter, and the beginnings of something real.

Chapter 29 – Community Response

The bell above the bakery door rang like a cheerful chime letting in a crisp draft of morning air and the chatter of the street. Morgana adjusted the tray of fresh pastries she was carrying. They were glazed rolls still steaming from the oven and their sheen glimmered beneath the lantern light. *The Golden Spoon* always smelled inviting, but today it carried something extra. It was like a soft cinnamon sweetness that seemed to hang in the air like an embrace.

Evander was already out front wiping down a table with exaggerated care though Morgana suspected he was less interested in crumbs and more in the group of patrons trickling inside. Even though he would never admit it he was a bit of a busybody. His hair caught the sunlight in dark strands shining like obsidian and his apron which was tied begrudgingly at her insistence made him look less like a seasoned swordsman and more like a misplaced farmer. Somehow though the sight fit.

"Morning Morgana!" called Mistress Elwyn. She was a stout woman with a wide smile who bustled in with two grandchildren in tow. "I've been dreaming of your muffins all week."

Morgana smiled warmly at the old woman as she set the tray down on the counter. "Then I hope these live up to your dreams."

The children darted forward with their noses twitching and their eyes wide at the rows of pastries gleaming like jewels under glass. Evander leaned over the counter, offering them a conspiratorial wink as though granting access to some secret treasure. One of the girls giggled, whispering loudly to her sister, "He's always here now."

The remark should have cut Morgana to the quick. Weeks ago the thought of anyone noticing Evander's constant presence would have sent her into spirals of panic. But today though her cheeks warmed her chest didn't clench with dread. *They've noticed. Of course they've noticed. And yet... they don't sound cruel.*

She caught Evander's amused glance. His brow was arched in silent acknowledgment of the children's words. She quickly busied herself with arranging the rolls though a smile tugged at her lips.

By midmorning the bakery was bustling. The usual crowd of market-goers, apprentices on errands, and old neighbors filled the space with warmth and chatter. But something was different today. Instead of the idle talk of weather and harvest more and more conversations drifted toward Morgana and Evander.

"Did you hear?" murmured an elderly man to his companion near the hearth. "She finally got herself some help in the shop. And not just help. He watches her like a hawk watches a lamb."

The woman chuckled. "Lamb is she? More like a fox. Look at the way she bosses him about."

Morgana with her cheeks flaming pretended to measure flour at the back counter. *Fox. Hawk. Saints preserve me they're dissecting us like characters from a play.*

Evander only grinned. He strode past, collected a tray of scones, and carried it out to the tables. His ease with the customers was remarkable. He crouched to help a child spread jam on a roll then straightened to discuss fencing with an apprentice boy who had recognized him from the training yards. All the while his presence was steady and natural like he had belonged here all along.

Mistress Elwyn cornered Morgana not long after. She leaned on the counter, her sharp eyes twinkling. "That one of yours then?"

Morgana nearly dropped the sugar scoop. "Mine?"

"Don't play coy girl. The way he looks at you you'd think the sun itself rose only to keep you warm."

Morgana stammered, He doesn't—*well not like—oh, saints what do I even say?* But her voice betrayed her before she found a defense. "He's… helpful."

Mistress Elwyn barked a laugh. "Helpful she says. A man doesn't tie on an apron and fetch jam for strangers unless his heart's been caught. Mark me lass no gossip's cruel in this. We're only glad to see you smile."

The words landed heavier than Morgana expected. For so long she had lived with the fear that discovery would mean condemnation, whispers, suspicion. Instead she found her neighbors only wanted her happiness. Warmth bloomed in her chest. It was fragile but growing.

Across the shop Evander caught her eye again. He raised his brows at her flustered look clearly curious about what had rattled her. She shook her head quickly, returning to her measuring. *He doesn't need to know everything they're saying. I'd never live it down.*

But oh the gossip refused to die down.

Later when Celeste popped in to collect her usual loaf two older patrons beckoned her over. "That friend of yours Morgana? She's finally let someone close has she?" one said in a hushed tone that wasn't hushed at all.

Celeste's smile widened wickedly. "Oh she'll pretend it's nothing. But just look at them. Sparks everywhere. About time if you ask me."

Morgana nearly choked on her own breath. *Celeste! Traitor!*

Celeste winked at her as she swept out with her bread leaving Morgana to face the knowing looks of half the shop.

Even Tomas who was usually her stalwart ally in discretion wasn't immune. He leaned on the counter between tasks smirking. "If you two keep this up then you'll be charging admission to the spectacle."

She glared at him, but he only chuckled and returned to sweeping.

It might have been unbearable if not for the tone behind it all. There was no venom and no malice. The whispers were laced with fondness, amusement, even hope. For a woman who had once feared the weight of any attention Morgana was stunned to find that the gaze of her community did not crush her. It lifted her even as it embarrassed her.

At one point a group of children gathered near Evander as he shaped rolls. "Make them into animals!" one demanded. "A rabbit! A bird!"

Evander with more confidence than skill twisted the dough into something vaguely resembling a rabbit. The children squealed with delight anyway and clutched the misshapen lumps as though they were treasures. Morgana shook her head but couldn't hide her grin.

He belongs here. Saints he really belongs here.

By evening as the last patrons trickled out Morgana leaned against the counter with a sigh brushing flour from her apron. Her cheeks ached from smiling all day. Evander joined her with his arms crossed over his chest, watching the golden glow fade from the windows.

"Busy day," he said with his voice low.

She nodded. "Louder than usual."

"You don't seem displeased."

"No," she admitted. "Not displeased." She hesitated then added, "They...noticed. Us."

His lips curved slowly. "Of course they did."

Her heart thudded. "And you're not bothered?"

He turned to her fully with his eyes warm and steady. "If the whole city wants to talk let them. I only care what you want Morgana."

Her throat tightened. She looked away blinking fast, but couldn't keep the smile from tugging at her lips. *What I want...maybe for once it's allowed to be simple.*

The bakery which was still faintly scented with sugar and spice seemed to breathe with her. It was a space no longer heavy with secrets but alive with comfort, laughter, and a community that embraced her happiness. For the first time Morgana let herself believe that being seen might not be dangerous at all.

That perhaps being seen could feel like love.

Chapter 30 – A Personal Challenge

The morning started like any other with flour dusting the air, ovens humming with heat, and the familiar cadence of customers outside the windows. But Morgana felt an uneasy coil in her stomach. Her latest recipe had seemed promising the night before. It was a honey–spiced loaf infused with a charm for calm and clarity. Simple, safe, something she thought even the bakery's walls would welcome.

But magic never stayed simple.

The loaves had risen beautifully with the golden-brown crusts gleaming in the oven's heat. At first she had breathed a sigh of relief. Then the scent began to thicken. It was sweet but cloying and sticky in the air like too much perfume. Her temples throbbed.

Something was wrong.

The dough on the cooling racks shivered. Not the natural crack of cooling crust, but a pulse like a heartbeat. Morgana's breath caught. *No. No, no, no.*

She whispered a quick counter-spell under her breath. But the loaves quivered harder and the honey glaze bubbled and dripped down their sides like molten amber.

Evander stepped into the kitchen just in time to see one of the loaves *jump*.

"Morgana?" His voice was wary though touched with the incredulity of a man who had seen more than his share of battle but never a loaf of bread try to escape.

She grimaced. "Don't panic. I can fix it."

"Not panicking," he said though his hand instinctively brushed the hilt of the knife at his belt. "But that bread just moved."

"It's not supposed to," she muttered through clenched teeth. She traced sigils in the air with her fingers, but the charms fizzled out like static. The loaves shuddered in response.

Then with a series of soft *plops* they rolled right off the cooling racks.

"Morgana!"

"I know!" she snapped as she lunged after one. It squirmed out of her grasp and it's warm crust was slick with honey. She nearly collided with Evander as another loaf hit the floor and *scuttled* under the table.

"This is—" Evander began, ducking to avoid a spray of sugar.

"Not normal," Morgana finished grimly. She slapped her palms together trying to weave a panicked dampening charm. The magic sparked and sputtered then burst outward in a puff of cinnamon-scented smoke.

The loaves responded as if delighted by the chaos. One rolled straight into a sack of flour and subsequently bust it open. White powder filled the air in a blizzard coating Morgana, Evander, and every surface in sight. Another loaf leapt onto the counter and began hopping like a frog.

Evander coughed through the haze. "Is this typical of your experiments?"

Morgana shoved hair from her face with her eyes watering. "No! Well. Sometimes. But not like this." Her heart hammered. *I can't let this get worse. If the wrong person sees...*

Another loaf bounced toward the door. Evander intercepted it and caught it in both hands like a wayward ball. He held it gingerly as he looked at it warily. "It's...alive."

"Not alive," Morgana corrected him as she rushed to bind it with a strip of enchanted parchment. "Just overly animated. The spell's gone sideways."

"Sideways?" His tone was somewhere between disbelief and laughter.

"Help me herd them before they cause more damage," she said desperately.

To his credit he didn't argue. Together they dashed after the rogue loaves. Morgana muttered binding charms as she lunged while Evander used sheer reflexes and battlefield precision to block their escape routes. At one point he dived under a table and emerged with two loaves pinned under his arm. He looked very triumphant despite the flour streaking his hair.

"Don't say it," Morgana panted as she struggled to stuff another wriggling loaf back into a pan.

"I wasn't going to," he said innocently though his grin betrayed him.

The chaos stretched on. Loaves bounced around, honey dripped, and sugar exploded from jars as if the bakery itself had joined in the rebellion. Morgana's frustration rose like steam. *I should be able to fix this. I should have controlled it before it spread. I can't keep making these mistakes.*

Her magic wavered with her panic. The loaves sensed the weakness hopping faster and then scattering like mischievous children.

Then Evander caught her wrist. His touch was firm. His eyes which looked steady and calm met hers. "Breathe. You're trying to chase them all at once. Focus."

She froze with her chest heaving. His words cut through the chaos slicing it down to something manageable.

"Pick one thing," he said quietly. "Anchor it. Then the next."

Her pulse steadied. She nodded. "Okay."

Together they cornered the nearest loaf. Morgana centered herself, whispered a gentler charm, and wove the silver thread into a lattice of calm. The loaf sagged with its wild twitching softening into stillness.

"Good," Evander murmured. He released her wrist, but his nearness lingered.

They worked like that. They targeted one loaf at a time together. Morgana wove. Evander blocked and caught. Their movements fell into rhythm as though they had done this a hundred times before. With each success her confidence rebuilt. With each glance his steady presence reminded her she wasn't alone.

Finally the last loaf collapsed in her hands harmless once more. Morgana sank onto a stool with her chest aching from exertion and her hair was matted with flour and honey.

Evander leaned against the counter beside her. His strong arms were crossed and his face just as dusted. For a long moment neither spoke. Then he chuckled low and warm.

"Well," he said, "I've fought men twice my size, but I've never battled bread before. I think this might have been harder."

A laugh burst from Morgana startled but genuine. She pressed her hands to her face as her shoulders shook. Relief washed through her mingled with exhaustion and something dangerously like joy.

When she lowered her hands Evander was watching her. His grin softened into something tender. "You're incredible you know that? Even when things go wrong you make it work."

Her breath caught. She wanted to argue and to confess that she felt like a mess of failures stitched together, but the sincerity in his gaze made the words stick in her throat.

Instead she whispered, "I couldn't have done it without you."

"Good," he said simply. "Because I'm not going anywhere."

Her heart ached with something fierce and sweet. *Not going anywhere.* She let the words settle deep like a promise.

The bakery was an absolute disaster with flour coating every surface, honey dripping down the counters, sugar scattered like starlight. But for once Morgana didn't feel ashamed of the mess. She felt proud. Because they had faced it together.

And in that chaotic sticky ruin she saw the shape of something steadier than fear. It was something that looked very much like love.

Chapter 31 – Emotional Milestone

The bakery was quiet again. Too quiet perhaps after the chaos of living bread and sticky honey storms. Flour still lingered in corners like fine snowfall and the scent of cinnamon clung stubbornly to the rafters, but the air itself felt...steady.

Morgana sat at the worn oak table in the back room brushing dried honey from her sleeves. Every muscle in her body ached from laughter, panic, and the stubborn effort of forcing magic back into line. She should have been exhausted to the point of collapse. But she wasn't.

She was waiting.

Evander had gone to check the door to make sure none of the enchanted loaves had escaped into the village. She pictured one bouncing into the marketplace and sending rumors flying before she had even caught her breath. But the door had remained shut and so had the world.

When he returned he didn't carry flour or bread. He carried silence. And the silence was heavier than any sack of sugar.

Morgana's heart stuttered. She had been bracing herself for this moment ever since she had admitted the truth to him. The whole truth about her magic, her mistakes, and her fears. She had imagined a hundred ways this could go. But now with him standing in the doorway with his hair mussed with flour and his eyes impossibly steady all her rehearsed words evaporated.

Evander crossed the room and lowered himself into the chair opposite hers. The wood creaked beneath his weight. He leaned forward with his fingers curling against each other as though he was working through some thought he hadn't dared speak until now.

"Morgana," he said at last.

Her breath caught. *It's happening. Whatever he says. It's happening now.*

"I've been turning this over in my mind." His voice was low and deliberate as though each word had to be chosen carefully. "Ever since you told me about the magic, about what you've carried, what you've feared. And especially after today when I saw you fight chaos itself and still find laughter at the end of it."

She wanted to speak, but her lips refused to part.

He drew in a steadying breath. "I've realized something. It doesn't matter how much I think about it or how many arguments I try to line up in my head. The truth is simple even if it terrifies me. I care for you. More than I ever expected to. More than I can keep to myself any longer."

The words seemed to hang in the flour-dusted air, glowing brighter than candlelight. Morgana's pulse roared in her ears.

He pressed on perhaps fearing her silence. "When I first stepped into this bakery, I never imagined I'd find a place that felt like home. Or a woman who made me laugh even in my darkest moods. But you...you've undone me Morgana. Every day and every moment I spend here I feel lighter. As though I'm no longer carrying everything alone. And I don't want to go back to the way I was before."

Her throat tightened. A thousand emotions clashed inside her. Fear, wonder, longing, and disbelief. For so long she had convinced herself that her magic would always mark her as dangerous and as unworthy of closeness. That the best she could do was keep her distance, keep her secrets, keep her heart locked away.

And yet here was Evander. Seeing all of her. Choosing her anyway.

Her fingers trembled against the table. "Evander…"

He looked up. His eyes searched hers looking raw and unguarded. "If this is too much and if it's not what you want then I'll stay quiet. But I couldn't keep it in any longer. I had to tell you."

Something inside her cracked wide open like the first rays of dawn breaking through a storm. Relief surged through her. It was so sharp it made her eyes sting.

"It *is* what I want," she whispered as the words tumbled out before she could swallow them down. "More than I can explain."

The tension in his shoulders broke. His lips parted, and the faintest smile curved his mouth. It looked hopeful, disbelieving, aching.

"You mean that?"

She nodded fiercely with her hands clutching at the edge of the table. "I've been afraid Evander. Afraid of hurting you and of hurting anyone. Afraid that if I let myself love it would all end in disaster. But today-" Her voice faltered. She steadied it with a breath. "Today I realized something. I don't have to do this alone anymore. And I don't want to. I want you. Exactly as you are. Exactly as this is."

The silence that followed was no longer heavy. It was electric.

199

Evander reached across the table. His hand hovered hesitantly as though offering her one last chance to retreat. She didn't. She slid her hand into his naturally. Their fingers threaded together as though they had always been meant to.

The warmth of his touch spread through her, chasing away the last lingering ghosts of fear.

For a long time they sat like that. No words, no spells, no pretenses just two hands clasped tight and two hearts pounding in rhythm.

Finally he broke the quiet. His voice sounded softer than she had ever heard it. "Do you have any idea how strong you are? How much I admire you?"

She laughed shakily, brushing at the tears that blurred her vision. "Strong? You just wrestled a loaf of enchanted bread into submission. I think you've got me beat."

His smile widened slow and warm. "Then maybe we're strong together."

The phrase sent a shiver through her not of fear but of certainty. *Strong together. Yes. That was exactly what they were.*

When he leaned closer she met him halfway. The kiss was gentle, tentative, and flavored faintly of flour and honey. But beneath its softness was a promise. A promise of safety, of honesty, of something lasting.

Once they parted her forehead rested against his. She could feel his breath against her lips steady and sure.

"I love you," he murmured. The words were simple and unadorned.

Her heart clenched. She had thought those words would terrify her, that they would demand too much, that they would reopen every wound she had tried to bury. But instead they filled her with a fierce aching relief.

She smiled through fresh tears. "I love you too."

The world seemed to exhale with them. Outside the city carried on with its hum of life unaware of the milestone reached within the bakery walls. The ovens still held the warmth of the morning. And though flour clung to every surface and sugar sparkled in every corner Morgana felt for the first time in years perfectly clean.

Loved.

Whole.

She lifted her head grinning through her tears. "Though we're going to need a whole day to scrub this place."

Evander laughed. The sound was so rich and unguarded. "Then we'll scrub it together."

And in that messy magical kitchen amid the ruins of their chaos Morgana felt her heart finally settle into peace.

Chapter 32 – Festival of Flavors

The town of Eraldor came alive in bursts of color, sound, and scent. Banners of scarlet, gold, and violet fluttered from lampposts as their threads caught the afternoon sun as though stitched with light itself. The cobblestone streets were crowded with stalls draped in bright cloth each overflowing with food, crafts, and delights that promised indulgence.

It was the Festival of Flavors. A yearly celebration the city held every autumn when the harvest was abundant and kitchens spilled over with creativity. Families walked hand in hand, children darted between booths clutching candied apples and roasted chestnuts, and music wove through the air light and playful.

For Morgana Valehart the air was thick not only with cinnamon, roasted nuts, and sugar but with nerves.

She stood behind her carefully prepared stall with its sign painted in soft golden script: *The Golden Spoon*. On the wooden counter trays of pastries gleamed like jewels: sugar-dusted scones, glossy tarts, biscuits swirled with jam, and at the center was her pride and a complete gamble. Muffins infused with carefully harnessed magic.

She wanted to subtly show people that magic in food wasn't automatically bad. She knew that people often liked her muffins and worked hard to make sure that the magic in them was very approachable for people. Her goal was to draw people in and make them comfortable not to create any concerns or problems.

The muffins didn't float, sparkle, or sing. She had worked too hard to ensure they were subtle. A touch of warmth lingered after a bite like sunshine spreading through the chest. The jam swirled more evenly than any ordinary hand could manage with every line neat and pleasing to the eye. And each pastry carried the faintest glow. It wasn't literal, but perceptible in the way people's faces softened when they looked at them.

For the first time Morgana wasn't hiding.

Evander stood at her side steady as a stone. He had helped haul the crates and set the table, brushing flour from his hair with an embarrassed laugh when she fussed over his shirt. Now he simply stayed close. His hand brushed hers when nerves made her fidget with the edge of the tablecloth. His presence was grounding like a hearth on a stormy night.

"You're trembling," he murmured just for her.

"I'm fine." She wasn't. Her heart raced like a trapped bird. *What if they notice? What if they feel it and panic? What if I ruin everything?*

He gave her one of those looks that was part amused and part unwavering. "You'll be more than fine. You'll be brilliant."

Before she could respond the first customer arrived.

A little girl with curly hair and a smear of chocolate across her cheek peered over the counter. Her father stood behind her smiling encouragingly. "Go on Elsie. Choose one."

The girl's eyes widened at the array of pastries. After a long moment of deliberation she pointed at a raspberry tart. Morgana handed it over to the girl forcing her hands not to shake.

Elsie bit into it. Her cheeks puffed with jam. Then her eyes lit up and she clapped her sticky hands together. "It tastes like...like happy!"

Her father laughed softly looking embarrassed but clearly delighted. "She means it's very good." He bought two more and led her away with Elsie already reaching for another bite.

Morgana exhaled shakily. That had been her first test. And it had not ended in disaster.

More customers followed. An elderly woman in a shawl bought a scone and declared it the softest she'd ever tasted. A group of apprentices purchased half a dozen muffins and ate them immediately on the curb, laughing between mouthfuls with crumbs dusting their sleeves. A pair of children pressed their noses to the counter until their mother relented and bought them jam biscuits which they ate while spinning in delighted circles.

Each time Morgana braced herself for suspicion, for narrowed eyes, and whispered accusations. But none came. Instead she saw smiles bloom, shoulders loosen, and laughter ring louder than before.

The magic was working but not in a way that frightened people. It enhanced what was already there. It didn't take choice away. It gave back comfort, steadiness, small joy.

And as the line grew her own fear shrank.

By midafternoon her tray of muffins was nearly empty. She wiped her brow with the back of her sleeve. She was flushed not only from the heat of the ovens earlier but from the sheer exhilaration of standing here in public, unhidden, and accepted.

"Miss Valehart!"

She looked up. A cluster of townsfolk approached the stall. They were faces she recognized as regular patrons of *The Golden Spoon*. Tomas was among them, looking tall and cheerful as always. He carried a mug of cider in one hand and waving with the other. "You're the talk of the festival. Everyone says your table is the one to try."

Her cheeks burned. "I—oh. Thank you."

Aurelia and Celeste appeared behind him weaving through the crowd. Aurelia's clever smile shone with her braid swinging as she approached. "I told you people would adore your baking if you let them see it as it truly is. Didn't I say so?"

Celeste who was carrying what looked like three skewers of candied fruit nearly dropped one in her eagerness. "It's true! You've got a crowd bigger than the roasted nut cart. That never happens." She grinned, eyes sparkling. "Also I may have been bragging to strangers that I'm your friend. That helped."

Morgana laughed. It was an unsteady but real laugh. Relief cracked through her nerves like sunshine splitting clouds. Her friends crowded around her teasing and praising and the festival no longer felt like a trial. It felt like celebration.

Music swelled nearby. She could hear the melody from a fiddler striking up a fast tune as dancers whirled in the square. The scent of spiced cider mingled with fried dough. It was sweet and warm. Lanterns were being strung overhead with golden light glowing against the darkening sky.

Evander leaned close. His voice was almost lost beneath the music. "Look around you Morgana."

She did.

Everywhere she turned people were eating her pastries. A young couple broke a tart between them, laughing as the filling stained their fingers. An elderly man savored a scone as if it were a treasure. Children licked jam from their palms and shouted with glee.

None of them looked afraid. None of them whispered accusations. They were simply…happy.

Her throat tightened. Pride swelled inside her fierce and trembling. For the first time she felt not like someone hiding at the edges of a world that would never accept her but like part of it.

She whispered mostly to herself, "I never thought this would be possible."

Evander's hand brushed hers beneath the counter. It was steady and sure. "I did."

Her heart thudded. She turned to him, but she felt the words catching in her chest. Before she could speak a group of children rushed up clamoring for more biscuits. She laughed breathlessly and bent to serve them with her movements lighter now and her shoulders no longer weighted by fear.

The evening deepened. Lanterns glowed brighter, the music grew wilder, and the line at her stall didn't shrink until the last tray was empty. Morgana stood there with flour on her hands, sugar streaked across her cheek, and her apron wrinkled and jam-stained and she felt triumphant.

When the final customer left licking crumbs from his fingers Morgana sagged back into her chair. Exhaustion washed through her, but so did joy. Pure unshakable joy.

Her friends crowded close with Aurelia squeezing her hand and Celeste already plotting next year's menu ideas. Tomas toasted her with his cider nearly spilling it in his enthusiasm.

Evander stood at her side with his hand warm against her back. He didn't speak. He didn't need to. His steady presence was enough.

Morgana looked at the lanterns glowing above and at the bustling square filled with laughter and music. She let the feeling of pride settle deep in her bones. For once she wasn't just surviving. She was celebrating.

She was part of the world again.

And for the first time in years she felt she belonged.

Chapter 33 – Magical Balance

The morning after the Festival of Flavors dawned quiet as though the whole city were still resting from its night of revelry. The streets were still strewn with bits of confetti while the faint scent of roasted nuts lingered in the air and colorful banners sagged from poles in weary triumph.

Inside *The Golden Spoon* the hush felt different. It felt peaceful and not tense. The ovens were warm again, the counters scrubbed, and the shelves restocked, but Morgana felt none of the old dread that usually followed a day of exposure.

For the first time in her life she had stood before the community as herself magic and all and been completely embraced. No whispers of witchcraft, no muttered accusations, no fear. There was just smiles, full bellies, and laughter.

And she wasn't about to let that trust be squandered.

Morgana stood at the worktable. Her sleeves were rolled back and her hands were pressed into a mound of dough. She moved slowly and carefully the way her mother had taught her long ago. Not just for the dough's sake, but for the magic.

The spell wasn't woven in haste nor hidden in secrecy. It was a deliberate choice. It was a soft thread of energy she nudged into the flour and butter with whispered words under her breath. *Let this bring warmth, but never bind. Let this comfort, but never compel. Let choice remain always.*

She released the dough with a breath that felt like a prayer.

Evander leaned against the doorframe watching her. He had been quiet all morning, letting her settle into the work at her own pace. Now he smiled faint but sure.

"You look different," he said.

Her lips quirked at one side. "Covered in flour again?"

"More than that." He crossed the room, brushing a stray lock of hair from her forehead. "You look steady. Like you're not carrying the same weight anymore."

Morgana's chest tightened, but not in the painful way it once had. She glanced down at the dough. At her fingers tracing the gentle folds of the mixture. "Maybe I'm not. Yesterday showed me something I hadn't let myself believe before. That magic doesn't have to be shameful or dangerous if I use it with care. That people can still see me, not just the spell."

Evander's gaze softened. "I saw you before. But I'll admit that I see you even more clearly now."

Heat rose in her cheeks. She ducked her head, but a smile still softened her lips.

They worked side by side preparing trays for the morning customers. Morgana found herself weaving in touches of magic with confidence she'd never dared before. They were all subtle, safe, and ethical. A loaf that browned evenly without burning. A tart whose filling held together neatly. A batch of biscuits that cooled faster than usual and ready just in time for the first customers.

Nothing flashy. Nothing binding. Just small kindnesses that made the work lighter and the food shine a little brighter.

When Aurelia came in for her usual morning tea she sniffed appreciatively. "Something smells especially balanced today."

Morgana nearly dropped her spoon. Aurelia's eyes twinkled knowingly, but she said nothing more. She only offered a smile and sipped her tea.

Celeste tumbling in a moment later with hair undone and a basket of wildflowers plopped herself onto a stool. "If you ask me yesterday's festival was just the start. You should always let your magic peek through. It's like sprinkles. Everything's better with them."

Morgana laughed, feeling the tension easing from her shoulders. The old fear would have bristled at those words, but now they felt like a blessing.

As the morning wore on the bakery filled with familiar faces. Customers lingered longer than usual, chatting warmly with Evander at the counter, and offering Morgana praise for the pastries they had devoured at the festival. No one asked for an explanation. No one accused. They simply enjoyed.

And Morgana finally enjoyed too.

When the last customer left Evander locked the door and returned to her side. She was washing her hands and humming under her breath when he set a gentle hand against her back.

"You know," he said, "I thought I admired you before. For your baking. For your kindness. For your determination to keep going even when you thought you had to hide. But now..."

She froze with water dripping from her fingers into the basin. "Now?"

"Now I admire you even more." His voice was firm and certain. "You've faced everything that frightened you and instead of running from it you've chosen to master it. Not just your magic, but yourself. You're stronger than you realize."

Her throat tightened, but this time the tears that pricked her eyes were warm and not bitter. She turned to him searching his face and saw nothing but truth there.

Slowly she dried her hands and reached for his. Their fingers laced together steady and sure.

"I couldn't have done it without you," she whispered.

"You could have," he countered gently. "But I'm glad you didn't have to."

The simplicity of the words undid her. She leaned into him resting her head against his chest and listening to the steady beat of his heart. It felt like the anchor she had always needed and the wings she had never dared to hope for.

For a long while they stood in the flour-dusted kitchen wrapped in each other's quiet. No chaos, no fear, no hiding. Just balance.

Morgana lifted her head. Her eyes shined with certainty. "I think," she said softly, "I've finally found the way to use magic that would have made my family proud."

Evander brushed a hand down her cheek reverent. "I think they would be very proud indeed."

Her smile trembled, but it was steady at its core. She felt whole. She felt seen. And she felt at last at peace.

The ovens crackled softly behind them carrying the scent of fresh bread into the quiet morning. Magic hummed faintly in the air. It wasn't wild or dangerous, but woven gently into the life they were building. It was safe, intentional, and balanced.

Together.

Chapter 34 – Quiet Moments

The Golden Spoon smelled of honey and cinnamon though the ovens had long been turned off for the evening. Candles flickered in their glass jars along the bakery's windowsill throwing warm uneven light across the wooden tables. Outside twilight softened into night as the streets were quiet except for the occasional cart's wheel clattering over cobblestones.

Morgana sat at one of the small tables with her hands cupped around a steaming mug of tea. The heat seeped into her palms and rose in little curls of fragrant steam. She detected mint, chamomile, and the faint sweetness of dried apple peel. Across from her Evander leaned back in his chair with his legs stretched out comfortably with one ankle hooked over the other. A rare expression of ease softened his usually sharp features.

For a while they didn't speak. There was no need. The hum of silence between them was companionable. It was the sort that comes only when both people have settled into each other's presence without expectation. Morgana stared at her tea, watching ripples tremble on its surface, and allowed herself the smallest smile.

Who would've thought I'd find peace in something so ordinary? Just tea, a table, and him.

Evander broke the quiet first. "You always look like you're plotting when you stare at your tea that way." His voice carried amusement low and warm.

She laughed softly shaking her head. "Not plotting. Thinking."

"Dangerous," he teased. His grin widened when she nudged his foot beneath the table.

"I could say the same about you," she retorted.

The banter was light and easy with threads weaving into a tapestry of comfort. But beneath it Morgana felt something sturdier than ease. There was a deepening trust and a quiet knowing that she could exist here without performance and without fear.

After a few sips she set her mug aside. "Do you miss it?" she asked suddenly.

Evander raised a brow. "Miss what?"

"Traveling. Adventure. Whatever it was you did before you started spending all your time here."

For a moment he considered her words. His eyes were half-lidded and his expression contemplative. "Sometimes. There's a thrill in movement. In seeing what lies beyond the next hill or city wall. But… adventure has its cost." His voice dropped a little. "And lately I've found more worth in staying put."

Her chest tightened at that. She didn't need to ask what he meant. His gaze lingered on her long enough to answer it without words. Heat curled through her cheeks and she busied herself with her mug again.

The sound of rain tapping against the windows broke the stillness. They both turned to look. The drizzle had come suddenly scattering silver drops across the glass panes. The bakery's sign outside swayed gently as the painted spoon caught faint glimmers of the soft lamplight.

"I love the rain," Morgana murmured.

"Of course you do," Evander said, voice full of gentle teasing. "It's cozy like everything else you surround yourself with."

She tilted her head at him. "And you don't?"

He shrugged, but his smile betrayed him. "Maybe I do. Especially when I'm in here instead of out there."

They sat like that until the rain grew heavier as the rhythmic patter settled into the background like a lullaby. Then Evander rose and disappeared into the kitchen. Morgana tilted her head curiously as she heard the faint clatter of crockery. When he returned he carried a plate with two slightly lopsided slices of honey-cake. Something she had baked earlier that day.

"You're stealing from my bakery stock?" she asked mock-scandalized.

He placed the plate between them completely unfazed. "Baker's privilege isn't it? And besides you didn't eat earlier. Too busy fussing over the custards."

She rolled her eyes though warmth pooled in her chest at his noticing. "You sound like an old nanny."

"Then eat before I start scolding like one," he said with mock sternness pushing the plate closer.

She broke off a piece and tasted it. The honey was mellow, the crumb soft, and though she had baked it herself it felt different sharing it this way. With Evander watching her with quiet satisfaction as though her enjoyment mattered to him. Which she realized it did.

When she reached for another bite he reached too. Their fingers brushed against each other on the plate. Neither pulled away immediately. His skin was warm against hers, feeling calloused but gentle. She met his gaze and for a suspended heartbeat the rain outside seemed to hush.

Morgana's pulse fluttered. She withdrew her hand first. A faint smile tugged at her lips to cover the rapid beat of her heart. *I could get used to this... I already am.*

Later after the cake was gone and their tea mugs emptied Evander suggested a walk. The rain had softened to a drizzle again. It was more mist than storm and the streets glistened under lamplight as though dusted with stars.

Morgana tugged her shawl around her shoulders, stepping beside him as they left the bakery. Cobblestones gleamed slick beneath their boots and water trickled in narrow streams along the edges of the street. The air smelled of wet stone and distant hearth smoke.

They didn't go far. Just around the block and past shuttered shops and a fountain whose stone cherub spat rainwater instead of clear water tonight. Evander slowed his pace deliberately as though savoring every moment. Morgana matched it with her hand brushing his now and again as they walked.

"Do you ever wonder," she asked quietly, "if this is all too simple for us? After everything?"

His brow furrowed slightly. "Simple doesn't mean undeserving."

She let his words settle into her softening the doubt that sometimes crept unbidden. "I suppose I'm just... waiting for the world to remind us it's not always kind."

"It will," he admitted without hesitation. "But that doesn't mean we shouldn't take this while we have it."

They paused near the fountain. A lone lantern swung overhead casting light across his face. She studied him noticing how steady he seemed and how sure he seemed even with rain dampening his hair and dripping from his jaw. Something inside her loosened.

"I never thought I'd want this," she confessed. "The quiet. The ordinary. I always thought I had to keep running and keep hiding. But with you it feels safe enough to stop."

Evander reached for her hand this time threading his fingers through hers with a gentleness that belied his size. "Then stop," he said simply. "Stay. Let yourself have this."

Her throat tightened with her eyes stinging unexpectedly. She pressed closer to him not caring about the rain. He smelled faintly of spice and smoke and when he tilted his head down to meet her gaze she whispered almost too soft to hear, "I think I love this."

His lips curved. "Me too."

They stayed there hand in hand until the drizzle faded and the first stars blinked into the night sky.

Back in the bakery they hung their damp shawls and cloaks by the fire. Morgana fetched another pot of tea and Evander lit the last candle on the mantel. They settled onto the same bench this time shoulder to shoulder as though neither wanted the distance of a table between them anymore.

The night stretched on with no more confessions and no grand declarations only quiet laughter, shared warmth, and the soft understanding that love for all its complexities could sometimes be found most fully in the ordinary.

This, Morgana thought as she rested her head lightly against his shoulder, *is the kind of magic I never expected.*

And in the hush of the bakery with rain-softened air drifting in through the cracked window it felt like the truest spell she had ever cast.

Chapter 35 – Sweet Ending

The bakery breathed with quiet contentment. Morning light spilled through the high windows in soft golden ribbons catching on motes of flour still drifting in the air. The scent of warm bread and honey lingered even though the ovens were cooling and the steady hum of life outside was muted through the glass. She heard the creak of wagons, the chatter of neighbors, and the heavy clip of hooves.

Morgana stood at the counter fingertips dusted with sugar gazing around her bakery as though she were seeing it anew. *The Golden Spoon* had always been her refuge and her shield against the world. She had poured her grief into its walls, kneaded her loneliness into its loaves, and whispered her secrets into its steam. But now it was something else entirely.

It was a home not just for her, but for the pieces of joy she had thought forever lost.

She brushed her hands against her apron smiling faintly. Evander's laugh echoed from the back room. It was a low unguarded sound that never failed to warm her. He had insisted on carrying flour sacks in himself refusing her protests that she could manage. *Stubborn man.* She rolled her eyes affectionately but her chest tightened with something tender.

I thought I'd be alone forever. That magic had taken too much from me. That my family's ghosts would be my only company. And yet... here he is.

The bell over the door jingled and Mrs. Calloway entered wrapped in her ever-present shawl. Behind he two children darted in giggling and their noses already twitching at the scent of cinnamon. Morgana smiled greeting them warmly and then slipped into the rhythm she knew so well. Orders, coins, thank yous all flowed like a song she had sung a thousand times.

But today every note felt different. Because she wasn't singing alone anymore.

Evander joined her at the counter brushing flour from his sleeves. His presence was so natural now that it startled her to remember the days when he had been only a curious stranger, a patron too devoted, and a complication she had feared rather than embraced. He stood beside her as though he had always belonged there. His broad hand felt steady when hers trembled and his quiet words anchored her when storms rose.

By midmorning the rush had eased. The shelves were half-emptied and the air filled with satisfied chatter from the last lingering patrons. Morgana leaned against the counter tucking a stray curl behind her ear. Evander set down a tray and looked at her, brow raised.

"Tired already?" he teased.

"Not tired. Just... thinking." She hesitated then admitted softly, "How much has changed."

He didn't laugh this time. Instead his expression softened. "For the better I hope."

She nodded meeting his gaze. "For the better."

Silence stretched for a moment. It wasn't heavy but full and laden with everything they didn't need to say out loud.

Later when the bakery had emptied Morgana and Evander sat at their small corner table with mugs of tea. Rain had begun again outside tapping steadily against the windows, but inside all was warm and golden.

Morgana wrapped her hands around her mug, letting the heat seep into her palms. "Do you ever wonder," she asked quietly, "what would've happened if I hadn't told you the truth?"

Evander's eyes met hers steadily. "You would've told me eventually. You're not the kind of woman who hides forever."

Her throat tightened. *But I tried didn't I? I almost let fear steal everything.*

"You forgave me," she whispered.

"I didn't need to forgive you," he said simply. "You were afraid. You wanted to protect me. And when it mattered you chose honesty. That's what I'll remember."

Her chest ached with a rush of love so strong it almost frightened her. But it didn't crush her instead it lifted.

The day wound on in cozy rhythm. A small magical spark danced in the kitchen when she pulled a tray of muffins too quickly and Evander caught it with a laugh, brushing the harmless shimmer from his sleeve. "You'll never let this place be ordinary will you?" he asked her shaking his head fondly.

"Would you want it ordinary?" she teased back.

"Not if it means losing this," he answered.

And just like that with a simple exchange Morgana realized how fully her life had shifted. Her magic was no longer something to fear or hide. It was a gift. A living and breathing part of her she had learned to wield with care, with love, with trust.

Evening fell. The bakery's lamps glowed soft and amber, casting long shadows against the flour-dusted counters. The last crumbs had been swept, the ovens stilled, and the quiet stretched between them like a soft blanket.

Morgana stood at the doorway looking out at the cobblestones glistening beneath moonlight. Evander stepped behind her resting his hand lightly against her back. The warmth of his touch radiated through her steady and grounding.

She drew in a deep breath, letting it out slowly. *This is what growth feels like. Not loud or triumphant, but quiet. A slow unfurling. A soft arrival.*

"I used to think love was something that happened in stories," she admitted softly. "Not for people like me. Not for someone who's lost so much."

Evander's voice was low and steady. "And now?"

She turned her head toward him with a small smile curving her lips. "Now I know love doesn't erase the losses. But it makes the weight easier to carry."

His arm slipped around her shoulders, pulling her gently against him. She leaned into his warmth and the simple solidity of his presence.

Together they watched the night deepen and the bakery behind them glowing like a beacon in the quiet street.

Much later when the lamps were out and the moon rode high Morgana sat a little table tucked in the bakery's corner. A single candle flickered beside her as she opened a fresh ledger. Instead of numbers she wrote words.

This year began with grief. With fear. With walls built so high I thought no light would ever find me. But it ends with hope. With magic I no longer fear and with love I never thought possible. I am not the same woman I was when I baked alone. And tomorrow... tomorrow I will keep growing.

She paused and set down her quill. Her gaze drifted towards her room overhead the bakery where Evander now dozed. He probably had one arm flung lazily over the blanket with his chest rising and falling in slow rhythm. She was nervous but still excited to be in the same bed as him.

Morgana's lips curved. She closed the ledger and blew out the candle.

Tomorrow can wait. Tonight I have enough.

And with that thought she quietly climbed the stairs and then slipped beneath the covers beside him. The scent of spice and warmth clung to the sheets. She rested her head lightly against his shoulder closing her eyes.

The Golden Spoon was silent but alive and filled with the quiet hum of dreams, of growth, of magic and love.

And as sleep took her Morgana knew with steady certainty that the sweetest ending was only the beginning.

Epilogue – A New Dawn

The first light of dawn spilled across the cobbled streets of Eraldor painting the rooftops in shades of rose and gold. Morgana Valehart stood at the bakery's front window with her fingers wrapped loosely around a steaming cup of tea and watched the city stir awake. *The Golden Spoon* looked almost otherworldly in the soft morning glow. Its sign swayed gently in the breeze as though the whole building itself breathed with her.

She had thought once that dawn was only a prelude to the grind of another day. It was a march toward obligation, a fear of mistakes, and the heavy weight of expectation pressing down on her shoulders. But now? Now dawn was different. It was promise. It was renewal. It was the beginning of something that felt wholly her own.

The bakery had survived storms, secrets, and magical mishaps, and so had she. She stood there with her tea and her gaze lingered on the horizon, Morgana could almost see her old self fading into memory. The timid woman who had walked into Eraldor burdened with doubts and tethered by rules she didn't fully understand.

Behind her the kitchen hummed with quiet activity. Evander was already awake with his sleeves rolled and his hands dusted in flour as he worked with deliberate ease. He had insisted on preparing the first batch of pastries himself though Morgana suspected he enjoyed the simple act of being part of her ritual as much as she did.

"You're staring again," he teased her without looking up his voice was rough with the edges of morning but softened by affection.

"Am I not allowed to?" she countered lightly sipping her tea. "The sunrise is particularly pretty today."

He glanced at her then with flour streaked across his cheek. His grin was quick and sure. "I wasn't talking about the sunrise."

Heat rushed to her cheeks and she rolled her eyes though her heart warmed all the same. She had grown used to his banter and the way his words landed like gentle sparks against her ribs. A year ago she might have flinched from such intimacy afraid of what it might demand of her. Now she let herself bask in it.

Morgana set her tea aside and crossed the kitchen, pressing a hand to his arm as she leaned closer. "You'll burn the pastries if you keep distracting me like that."

"Ah but if I burn them I'll simply call it a new recipe," Evander replied leaning closer still.

The moment stretched soft and sweet before Morgana stepped back with a laugh. It felt good and necessary to laugh easily. To feel her chest loosen with something other than anxiety.

As the morning unfolded the first customers trickled into *The Golden Spoon*. Familiar faces. Every one of them. Old Maribel with her weathered shawl who swore the scones kept her arthritis at bay. The twins Cassia and Clem whose schoolbooks always ended up dusted with powdered sugar. Even the city guards made their rounds more often now, stopping by not only for bread but for a moment of warmth. A slice of belonging.

The bakery had become more than a business. It had become a hearth for the city itself. A place where magic and the mundane braided together without fear and where laughter mingled with the scent of cinnamon and caramelized butter. Morgana had not merely earned their acceptance, but she had become part of their lives as they had become part of hers.

And with that came responsibility. She knew the whispers still lingered. She heard quiet stories of the old bakery that had once twisted customers' choices with enchanted bread. But now when people spoke of magic in baking they spoke of her not as a cautionary tale, but as a symbol of balance and of careful deliberate trust.

One young boy tugged at her sleeve that morning, his eyes bright with admiration. "Miss Valehart when I grow up I want to bake with magic too."

Morgana crouched to meet his gaze. Her heart stirred with equal parts pride and protectiveness. "Then you must remember this. Magic is like sugar. A little can sweeten, but too much can spoil everything. Always bake with care and always with love."

The boy nodded solemnly as though she had entrusted him with a sacred secret. Perhaps in a way she had.

By midmorning the bakery was buzzing with laughter spilling into the street along with the scent of spiced rolls. Evander worked beside her. His hands were steady and his presence a quiet anchor. They moved in rhythm now a seamless dance born of trust and affection. Sometimes their eyes would meet over a tray of cookies and it was enough. It was an entire conversation without words.

Later when the rush eased and the last crumbs of breakfast pastries disappeared into the hands of contented patrons Morgana found herself back at the window. The sun was higher now gilding the city in bold light and she let her thoughts wander freely.

She thought of her journey. Of the first spell that had gone wrong, the shame of failure, and the long nights wondering if she had chosen the wrong path. She thought of the friendships forged, the laughter shared, the risks taken and survived. And she thought of Evander who was steady and stubborn who had stood beside her even when she wavered.

A new dawn she realized was not only about beginnings. It was about continuance. About choosing each day to rise again and meet the world with hope.

Evander came to stand beside her. His hand slipped into hers. "You're quiet."

"Just thinking," she murmured leaning lightly against him.

"Dangerous habit," he teased though his thumb brushed over her knuckles with tender gravity.

Morgana smiled faintly. "Do you ever think about what comes next?"

"Every day," he admitted. "But I find I'm less worried about the future than I used to be. Probably because I know I won't be facing it alone."

Her chest swelled as she felt emotion prickling at the corners of her eyes. She blinked it back and tightened her grip on his hand.

Together they watched as the city bustled into life with vendors calling out their wares, children darting through the square, and neighbors greeting neighbors with cheerful nods. The world was imperfect, it always would be, but it was beautiful in its imperfection.

And for the first time in her life Morgana Valehart did not feel like an outsider looking in. She was home.

The bell above the bakery door chimed again announcing another customer. But Morgana lingered at the window just a moment longer. Her heart lifted with a sense of quiet certainty.

Whatever tomorrow brought she would meet it with courage. With love. With magic that did not bind or burden, but set free.

A new dawn had come. And it was only the beginning.

Chocolate Chip Cookies

Yields: about 4 dozen small cookies

Ingredients
- 1 cup unsalted butter, softened
- ½ cup granulated sugar
- 1 cup packed brown sugar
- 2 eggs
- 2 teaspoons vanilla extract
- 2¼ cups all-purpose flour
- 1 teaspoon baking soda
- ½ teaspoon salt
- 2½ cups semisweet chocolate chips

Preparation

1.   Preheat oven to 350°F. Line baking sheets with parchment paper.

2.   In a large bowl cream together butter, granulated sugar, and brown sugar until smooth and fluffy.

3.   Beat in eggs one at a time then mix in vanilla extract.

4.   In another bowl whisk together flour, baking soda, and salt. Gradually add dry ingredients to wet mixture until just combined.

5.   Stir in chocolate chips.

6.   Drop rounded spoonfuls of dough onto prepared baking sheets, leaving space between cookies.

7.   Bake for 8–10 minutes or until edges are golden while centers remain soft.

8.   Let cookies rest on the baking sheet for 2 minutes then transfer to a wire rack to cool completely.

Honey Cinnamon Challah

Yields: about 3 loaves

Ingredients
Dough:
- 1 tablespoon yeast
- 1¼ cups lukewarm water
- 5 cups all-purpose unbleached flour
- ½ cup granulated sugar
- 1 tablespoon ground cinnamon
- ½ tablespoon salt
- ¼ cup honey
- ¼ cup vegetable oil
- 2 eggs

Topping:
- 2 eggs + 1 teaspoon water
- 1 tablespoon ground cinnamon

Preparation
1. In a small bowl, combine yeast, 1 teaspoon sugar, and lukewarm water. Stir gently and let sit for 10 minutes until foamy.
2. In a large bowl or stand mixer whisk together flour, salt, cinnamon, and the remaining sugar. Reserve some flour for kneading.
3. Add yeast mixture, oil, eggs, and honey. Mix thoroughly.
4. Knead in the reserved flour, working the dough until smooth and no longer sticky for about 10 minutes.
5. Place dough in a lightly greased bowl and cover with a damp towel then let rise for 1 hour.

6.   Preheat oven to 350°F.

7.   Divide dough into portions, braid or shape as desired, and place on a parchment-lined baking tray. Get creative!

8.   Let rise another 30 minutes.

9.   Beat eggs with water. Brush over challah and sprinkle with cinnamon.

10.   Bake for 25 minutes or until golden brown. Cool before slicing.

Acknowledgements

This book found its way to the page because of the many hands and hearts that believed in it along the journey. Every step from the earliest spark of an idea to the last line written was sustained by encouragement, patience, and trust. The quiet moments of doubt were softened by kindness and the long stretches of work were brightened by unexpected inspiration. To everyone who gave this story space to grow and room to breathe you are part of its foundation. And to every reader who lets these words take root in their own imagination I offer my deepest gratitude.

www.ingramcontent.com/pod-product-compliance
Lightning Source LLC
Chambersburg PA
CBHW031323170626
46807CB00002B/542